Edmund Hodgson Yates

Dr. Wainwright's Patient

A novel. Vol. 2

Edmund Hodgson Yates

Dr. Wainwright's Patient
A novel. Vol. 2

ISBN/EAN: 9783337213602

Printed in Europe, USA, Canada, Australia, Japan

Cover: Foto ©Andreas Hilbeck / pixelio.de

More available books at **www.hansebooks.com**

DR. WAINWRIGHT'S PATIENT.

A Novel.

BY

EDMUND YATES,

AUTHOR OF

"BLACK SHEEP," "WRECKED IN PORT," "BROKEN TO HARNESS," ETC.

"Canst thou not minister to a mind diseased,
Pluck from the memory a rooted sorrow,
Raze out the written troubles of the brain,
And with some sweet oblivious antidote
Cleanse the stuffed bosom of that perilous stuff
Which weighs upon the heart?"
                                        SHAKESPEARE.

IN THREE VOLUMES.

VOL. II.

LONDON:

CHAPMAN AND HALL, 193 PICCADILLY.

1871.

CONTENTS OF VOL. II.

———◆◆◆◆———

and disarranged a muslin scarf which she wore
round her shoulders, she saw that Mrs. Stothard
was busily engaged at a chest of drawers standing
in a somewhat remote corner of the room. Annette was silent, but she glanced stealthily and
shiftily out of the corners of her eyes. Mrs.
Stothard still remained immersed in her occupation. The girl shifted uneasily from one foot to
the other, hesitating, dallying; then shook herself
together, as it were, and seeing she was still unno-
ticed, with a low chuckle silently and swiftly passed
through the doorway and descended the stairs.

In seaside places such as Beachborough the
evenings in late summer are chilly. There was
a handful of fire in the dining-room grate, and
while Miss Annette was sulking upstairs, and de-
liberating whether she should or should not come
down, Captain Derinzy was standing on the rug
with his back to the grate, and from that post of
vantage was haranguing his wife and his guest—
Dr. Wainwright—in his own peculiar way. When
he was alone with his wife the Captain was silent
and submissive; when a third person was pre-

sent, and he knew that a curtain-lecture was the worst he had to dread, he was loquacious and imperative.

"And again I say to you, Wainwright," said he, in continuance of some previous conversation, "she's got to that pitch now that she isn't to be borne. I can stand a good deal—no man more so; they used to say, when I was on the Committee of the Windham, that I had a—a—what was it?—judicial mind; that was what they called it, a judicial mind—but I can't stand this girl and her tempers, and so something must be done; and there's an end of it, Wainwright!"

There are some men who are never called by any but their Christian names, and those often familiarly abbreviated, by their most promiscuous acquaintance. There are others in whose appearance and manners something forbids their interlocutors ever dispensing with their courtesy titles. Dr. Wainwright, one would have said, undoubtedly belonged to the latter class. He was a tall man, standing over six feet in height, with a high bald forehead, large features, square jaw, and deep piercing gray eyes. His manners were placidly courtly, his naturally sonorous voice was skilfully modulated, and there was an unmistakable air of latent strength about him, a sort of consciousness of the possession of certain power, you could not tell what. . He might have been a duke, or a philosopher in easy circumstances, or a " man in authority, having servants under him." Quiet, dignified, and bland, he held his own amongst all sorts and conditions of men, and with the exception of two or three intimates of a quarter of a century's standing, Captain Derinzy was probably the only person living who would have thought of calling him " Wainwright." The Doctor winced a little at the repetition of the familiarity, but beyond that took no notice of it.

"My dear Captain Derinzy," said he, after a moment's pause, " I can perfectly appreciate your feelings. I have not the least doubt that Miss Derinzy's unfortunate illness is the source of great annoyance to you. Still, if you are indisposed to run certain risks, which, as I have explained to Mrs. Derinzy—"

" I thought by this time, Dr. Wainwright," interrupted the lady, " you would have seen the utter futility of paying the least attention to any- thing which Captain Derinzy may say !"

" My love !" murmured the Captain.

" He is as fully impressed as any of us," con- tinued Mrs. Derinzy, without taking the least notice of her husband, " with the necessity of our pursuing the course we have agreed upon ; but he has a passion for hearing his own voice ; and as he knows that I never listen to him, he is only too glad to find some one who will."

" No, no ! Look here, Wainwright," said the Captain. " It's all very well, you know, but Mrs. Derinzy don't put the thing quite fairly. She's a woman, you know, and it's natural for women to be dull and left alone, and all that; but a man's a different thing. He requires—"

Captain Derinzy did not finish his sentence as to a man's requirements, for Dr. Wainwright's quick ear had caught the sound of an approaching footstep, and he held up his hand and raised his eyebrows in warning, only in time to stop his voluble host as the door opened and Annette appeared.

As she entered the room Dr. Wainwright immediately faced her. There was no mistaking his figure and presence, even if she had not expected to find him there. Nevertheless, her first idea was to close the door and run away. But she would scarcely have had the opportunity of doing this, however much she might have wished it; for the Doctor at once stepped across the room, and had taken her hand in his, and was bowing over it in his old-fashioned courtly way, almost before she was aware of it.

"There is no occasion to ask after your health, Miss Annette," he said in his soft pleasant tone. "One has only to look at you to have one's pleasantest hopes confirmed. You and the Dorsetshire air do credit to each other."

"I am quite well," said Annette shortly, taking her hand from his.

"Here's dinner!" said the Captain. "You see, we don't make a stranger of you, Wainwright —at least, Mrs. Derinzy doesn't. There's a dam prejudice in this house against using the drawing-room; so we sit stiving in this infernal place, 'parlour, and kitchen, and all,' and— Where will you sit?"

Sentence abruptly concluded in consequence of unmistakable manifestations of his wife's being unable to put up with him any longer.

"Thank you, Captain Derinzy, I'll sit over here, if you please," said the Doctor, with an extra dash of stiffness in his manner; "opposite Miss Annette; and, if you'll permit me, I will move these flowers a little on one side, that I may get a better view of her."

"Why do you always stare at me?" said Annette, with a defiant air.

"Do I stare?" asked Dr. Wainwright. "If I do, I am exceedingly rude, and ought to know better. But haven't you used the wrong word, my dear young lady? I look at you, perhaps; but I hope I don't stare."

"Looking and staring are all the same. I hate to be looked at!"

"You are the very first girl I ever heard give

utterance to that sentiment," said the Doctor cheerily; "and you'll soon outgrow such ideas."

"I daresay we shall hear no more of them after her cousin Paul has been staying with us," said Mrs. Derinzy. "We expect Paul soon now, Doctor."

"I have heard a good deal of Mr. Paul from my son, who is in the same office with him. They seem to be great allies, and George speaks in the highest terms of Mr. Paul."

"Is your son's name George?" asked Annette.

"Yes."

"Your own name is not George?"

"No; mine is Philip."

"I'm glad it is not the same as your son's."

The Doctor and Mrs. Derinzy exchanged glances, and were silent; but Captain Derinzy, who all his life had been notorious for his obtuseness in taking a hint, said:

"Why, what a ridick'lous thing you are sayin', Annette! Why are you glad the Doctor's son's name's not the same as his? What on earth difference could it make to you?"

"It could not make any difference to me," said the girl quietly; "only, I don't know why, I think I should wish to like Dr. Wainwright's son, and—and—"

"And the less he is like his father the greater the chance of your doing so; isn't that it, Miss Annette?" asked the Doctor, with his pleasant smile.

"Yes," said Annette, looking him straight in the face, "you're quite right; that is it."

This blunt communication was received by those who heard it after very different fashions. Mrs. Derinzy knit her brows, and, after looking savagely at her niece, shrugged her shoulders at the Doctor, as much as to say, "What could you expect?" Captain Derinzy laid down his knife and fork, and muttered, "O, dam!" apparently in confidence to his plate. The Doctor alone maintained his equanimity unimpaired. There was a pause—considering the tremendous character of the last remark a very short pause—and then he said:

"Now, there's an instance of the injustice

which is done by your sex, Mrs. Derinzy, to ours. Miss Netty, with an honesty which is *impayable*, and which, if there were a little more of it in polite society, would go far to the explosion of what Mr. Carlyle calls ' shams and wind-bags,' says she doesn't like me. She gives no reason, you observe ; so that I am relegated to the same position as another member of our profession — Dr. Fell — who also was misliked, and equally without reason alleged."

" I could tell you the reasons for my disliking you," said Annette.

It was extraordinary, the change which had come over her face. The cheeks were full-blooded, the eyes suffused and starting from her head, the hair pushed back, the whole look fierce and defiant.

" Could you ?" said the Doctor ; then, after looking up at her, adding very quickly, " Ah, but you must not. I don't want to hear a list of my shortcomings, or a catalogue of my faults. I'm too old to make up for the one or get rid of the other ; and— Mrs. Derinzy, I must congratulate you on your cook. It is rare indeed, in what I may be pardoned in calling these out-of-the-way regions, that one comes across anything like this *filet de sole*."

He turned his face towards his hostess as he said these words, and spoke in her direction, but he scarcely moved his eyes from direct contemplation of Annette. The girl's face, with the same flush on it, was looking down, and she seemed to be working nervously with her hands, rapidly intertwining and then separating them, under the table.

Captain Derinzy, at the Doctor's last remark, had given vent to a very curious sound, half-sigh of self-commiseration, half a grunt of contempt. He had not learned much in the half-century during which he had adorned life—his natural gifts had been small, and he had not taken much trouble to improve upon them—but one thing he had arrived at, and that was an appreciation of good cooking. He not merely knew the difference between good and bad dishes—in itself by no means a common acquirement—but he had a knowledge of the arcana of the art, and great high-priests whose temples were the kitchens of London clubs had taken his opinion on the merits of various *plats*.

" Well," he said, after a moment, " that's a funny thing! I know you, Wainwright. You're not the kind of fellow to go in for politeness, and all that kind of thing—I mean, of course, flummery, you know, and all that—and yet you say we've got a good cook, and this is nice *filet de sole!* Why, there are fellows used to tell you about doctors, you know—' O yes, it's all very fine,' they used to say, ' for doctors to tell you not to eat this, and not to drink that, and all the time they're regular *gourmets*, don't you know!' Well, I think that's all stuff, for my part. They may know all very well about broth and beef-tea, and all that sort of beastliness that they give people when they're getting better; but I only knew one of 'em that ever knew anything really about cooking, and he was an old fellow who'd been out in India, and was a C.B., or something of that sort; and he told the cook at the Windham how to make a curry—peculiar kind of thing, quite different from what you get mostly—that was delicious, by Jove! As for this stuff," continued the Captain, taking up a portion of the lauded *filet* on the end of his fork, and eyeing it with great disgust, " it's dry and tough and leathery, and tastes like badly-baked flannel-waistcoat, by Jove!"

During this speech Dr. Wainwright, although his polite attention to it had been obvious, had scarcely removed his glance from Annette. It remained on her as he said, turning his face in the Captain's direction, and laughing heartily:

" I never tasted badly-baked flannel-waistcoat, Captain Derinzy, and I still stand up for the excellence of the *filet*. However, I'm not going to be led into giving any opinion whether we're good judges of good living, or rather whether we exemplify the well-known exceptions which prove rules by not practising what we preach. But one thing can't be denied—that we hear of very curious stories about fancies in eating and drinking. I heard of one only the other day, of an old gentleman who had had the same breakfast for thirty years; and what do you think, Mrs. Derinzy, were its component parts?"

Mrs. Derinzy, also curiously observant of Annette, roused from her quiet watchfulness, and gave herself up to guessing. Tea, coffee, milk, cream, porridge, toast, ham, eggs, she suggested; while claret, brandy-and-soda, anchovy, devilled anything, and bitter beer in a tankard, were proposed by her husband. The Doctor shook his head at all these items, grimly saying:

" What should you say to Irish stew and hot whisky-and-water?"

" Heavens!" cried Mrs. Derinzy.

" For breakfast?" asked the Captain.

" For breakfast; and eaten in bed every day for thirty years!"

" O, dam!" said the Captain. " If you hadn't told the story, Wainwright, I shouldn't have believed it. Of course, if you say so, it is so; but the fellow must have been off his head—mad!"

Before he had uttered the last word Mrs. Derinzy, who seemed to have an idea of what was coming, had stretched out her hand towards her husband in warning, while even Dr. Wainwright moved uncomfortably on his chair. Had Annette heard it? Little doubt of that. She looked up slyly, very slyly, with a half-stealthy, half-searching glance at the Doctor; then raising her head, glared defiantly at her aunt, as though marking whether she were affected by the suggestion. She looked long and earnestly; then finding that Mrs. Derinzy's attention was concentrated on her, she withdrew her glance, and relapsed into her former stolid condition.

So the dinner progressed—pleasantly to Captain Derinzy, as a break in the monotony of his life. Not merely did Mrs. Derinzy, who, in her capacity of housekeeper, kept the keys of the cellar and exercised a rigorous economy in that department—not merely did she increase both the quality and quantity of the wine supplied to the table, but she refrained from joining in the conversation more than was absolutely demanded of her by politeness, and consequently the Captain was able to direct it into those channels which most delighted him. It is needless to say that

those channels ran with small-talk and fashion-
able gossip, and petty details of that London life
which he had once so thoroughly enjoyed, and
from which he was now so unwillingly exiled.
The Captain found his interlocutor perfectly able
to converse on these his favourite topics. One
might have thought that Dr. Wainwright had
nothing better to do than to flutter from club
to mess-room, and from mess-room to boudoir,
so well was he up in the *chronique scandaleuse*
of the day, adapting his phraseology, his voice,
and manner to the fashion of the times. The
Captain was delighted; great names, once fami-
liar in his mouth as household words, but the
mention of which he had not heard for ages, were
once more ringing in his ears; the conversation
seemed to possess the old smoking-room and
barrack flavour so dear to him once, so dead
to him of late; and while under its spell, his
manner renewed its ancient swagger and his
voice its old roll. He yet asked himself how
the man whom he had hitherto only known as
the sober sedate physician could have recalled

such sentiments or borne so essential a part in their discussion.

At length the Doctor's anecdotes commenced to flag, and the Doctor himself was obviously seeking for an opportunity of breaking off the conversation. Mrs. Derinzy, who had been apparently dropping off to sleep, roused up with the declining voices, and catching a peculiar expression in the Doctor's face, was on the alert in an instant. That peculiar expression was a glance towards Annette, accompanied by a significant elevation of the eyebrows, following immediately upon which Dr. Wainwright said,

"And now I must drop this charming conversation which we have had, my dear Captain Derinzy, and, falling back into my professional character, must declare that it is time for us to adjourn.—Beauty sleep, my dear Miss Netty"— walking quickly round and laying his hand lightly on her shoulder—lightly, though she quivered under the touch, and rose at once from her seat— "beauty sleep is not to be had after twelve, they tell us; and though you don't require it, and

though you said you didn't like to be looked at
—O, Miss Netty!—yet I think we're all of us
sufficiently tired to wish for it to-night. So good-
night! You don't mind shaking hands with me,
though you were cruel enough to say you disliked me; good-night. — Good-night, Mrs. Derinzy; you feel stronger to-night? Let me feel
your pulse for one moment." Then in a rapid
under-tone to her, " Do you go with her, while
I speak a word to Mrs. Stothard. Don't leave
till she returns." Again aloud, " Good-night."

The Captain was making a final foray among
the decanters as Mrs. Derinzy and Annette, closely
followed by Dr. Wainwright, passed out of the
door, immediately on the other side of which Mrs.
Stothard was standing. She was about to follow
the ladies, but a sign from the Doctor arrested
her, and she let them pass on, remaining behind
with him. He said but very few words to her,
and those in a muttered under-tone, but she understood them apparently, nodded her reply, and
hurried away upstairs.

"Now, Miss Derinzy, get to bed; do you hear? This is the last time I shall speak to you; next time I shall *make* you."

The tone in which these words are said is very unlike Mrs. Stothard's usual tone; but it is Mrs. Stothard's voice and it is Mrs. Stothard herself—equipped in a tight linen jacket fitting her closely and without any superfluity of material, and a short clinging petticoat—who is standing by the bed on which Annette is seated.

"Come, do you hear me?" she repeats, taking the girl by the shoulder; "undress now, and get into bed. We're ever so late as it is."

But the girl sits stolidly gazing before her, and never moving a muscle.

Then Mrs. Stothard bends down and looks into her face—looks long and earnestly, the girl never flinching the while—and comes back to her upright position, with her cheeks a little paler and her mouth a little more set.

"The Doctor was right," she mutters between her teeth; "there's one coming on to-night, and a bad one too, I fancy."

She goes to a drawer, takes out some article, and lays it on the bed hard by. The girl shoots a stealthy glance out from under her eyelids, sees what is done, sees what is fetched, and drops her eyes again on to the floor.

"You won't! you've heard me, you know, Annette! You won't undress! Come, then, you shall!"

Mrs. Stothard, bending over the girl, undoes the top button of her dress, the second button, the third. The fourth is not so easily undone, and Mrs. Stothard shifts her position, comes round, and kneels in front of her. Then, with a low long howl, more like that of a beast at bay than a human creature, the girl dashes at her throat and bears her to the ground. A bad time for the nurse, this. The attack is so sudden, that for one moment she is overpowered; the next her presence of mind returns, and with it her strength of wrist. Her hands are wound in the girl's long hair then floating down her back; she tears at it with all her force, until the distorted face, which had been glaring into hers, is wrenched backward, and under torture the hand-grip on her throat is relaxed. Then she slips herself from underneath her foe and closes with her. They are both on the ground, locked in each other's arms, and struggling furiously, what is more wonderful silently, for, save their deep breathing, neither emits a sound, when the door opens softly and Dr. Wainwright enters. Annette's face is towards him: her eyes meet his, and the wild rage dies out of them, to be succeeded by a glance of fear and horror; and her grasp relaxes and her arms fall helplessly by her sides, and she moans in a low voice,

"It is here again! O my God, it is here again!"

"And only here just in time, apparently, Mrs. Stothard," says the Doctor, helping the nurse to rise. "This is a very bad attack. Just assist me to put this on her," he added, taking the *camisole de force* from off the bed, and putting it over Annette's head as she sat rigid on the floor; "and keep it on all night, please. A very bad attack indeed."

"Bad attack!" said Mrs. Stothard; "I'm glad

you've seen it, Dr. Wainwright. You never would believe me before. But I've often told you, in all your practice you've got no worse case than that she-devil there. And yet these fools here think she will be cured!"

"Strong language, strong language, Mrs. Stothard," said the Doctor deprecatingly. "But I don't think you're far out in what you say; I don't, indeed!"

CHAPTER II.

A CONQUEST.

IT is the end of August, and society has gone out
of town. Sporting people have gone to Good-
wood; and the Lawn, at the period of our story,
as yet uninvaded by objectionable persons, pro-
mises to present, as it hitherto has always presented, a *parterre* of aristocratic beauty. There
is no " limited mail" in these days; but they could
tell you at Euston-square of seats for the North
booked many days in advance. And there are no
Cook's tourists; and yet it would seem impossible
that the boats leaving Dover twice a-day for the
great continental routes, *via* Calais and Ostend,
could possibly carry more passengers. That was
before the contemptible German system of *battues*
was allowed among us, when *dreib-jagds* were
almost unknown in England, and when a day's

shooting meant exercise, trouble, and skill, not
warm corners and wholesale slaughter; but Pur-
days and Lancasters, though mere muzzle-loaders,
did their work, and Grant's gaiters were to be
found on most of the right sort throughout the
English counties.

The physicians and the great surgeons have
struck work,—it is no good remaining in a place
where there are no patients,—and having delegated
their practice *pro tem.* to some less fortunate brother,—who devoutly prays that chance may bring
some rich or celebrated person unexpectedly to
town, then and there to be stricken with illness,
and left in his, the substitute's, hands,—they are
away shooting in the Highlands, swarming up
Swiss mountains, lounging at German Brunnen,
but never losing the soft placid manner and the
dulcet tone which seem to imbue their every
speech and action with a certain professional air,
as though they were saying, "Hum! ha! ye-es,
certainly; show me the tongue, please—ah!" and
wherever they may be, the scent of the hospital
is over them still.

Passing through Edinburgh, on his way to his shooting in Aberdeenshire, Mr. Fleem, President of the College of Surgeons, gives up a week of his hard-earned holiday to the society of Sir Annis Thettick, the great Scotch operator, and the pair indulge in many a sanguinary colloquy; little Dr. Payne leaves Mrs. Payne to be escorted up and down the *allées* of Baden-Baden by trim-waisted Prussian and Austrian officers, or by such of her compatriot acquaintances as she may find there (all of whom are too glad to pay court to so charming a woman), while he is closeted with Herr Doctor Von Glauber, Hof-Arzt to his Effulgency the reigning Duke of Schweinerei, with whom he exchanges the most confidential communications, resulting on both sides in a belief that the real knowledge of either of them is extremely limited.

In those charming courts and groves dedicated to the study and practice of the law there is also tranquillity, not to say stagnation, for the long vacation has commenced, and the Law is out of town.

Read the fact in the closed courts of Westminster Hall—in the Hall itself, no longer filled
with the anxious faces of suitors, the flying
forms of bewigged barristers, or fragrant with the
sprinkled snuff of agitated attorneys, but now
given up to marchings and counter-marchings of
newly-fledged volunteers, who—it is the first year
of the movement—are longing to be taking martial
exercise in the wilds of Wimbledon or on the
plains of Putney, but, deterred by the rain, are
fain to put up with the large area of Westminster
Hall, and to undergo the torture of the professional drill-sergeant before the eyes of a gaping
and a grinning audience.

Read the fact in the closed oaks of every
set of chambers, each door bearing its coffin-
plate - like announcement that messages and
parcels are to be left at the porter's lodge; in
the sounds of revelry that proceed from the attorneys' offices, where the scrubs left in town
are amusing themselves with effervescing drinks
and negro minstrelsy, oblivious of executors,
administrators, and hereditaments; while the

"chief" is at Bognor with his wife and children, the " Chancery" is geologising at Staffa, and the " Common-law" is living up at Laleham Ferry, and washing off all reminiscence of John Doe and Richard Roe in daily matutinal plunges off the bar at Penton Hook.

All the members of the Bar, great and small, are away. Heaven alone knows where the Great Seal may be hidden, but it is certain that the keeper of it and the Sovereign's conscience—a tall, straggling-whiskered, gray-haired gentleman—has been seen, with a wideawake hat on his head and a gun in his hand, "potting" rabbits on a Wilt-shire common, and has been pointed out seated in a dog-cart at a little railway-station as the " Lar' Chance'lar" to the wondering bumpkins, who fully expected to see him in full-bottomed wig and gold-fringed robes, and who were conse-quently wofully disappointed, and thought his lordship of but " little 'count." Tocsin the great gladiator, who wrestles with his professional oppo-nents and flings them heavily, cross-buttocks the jury, and has been known, metaphorically, to give

that peculiar British blow known as "one" to the
judge himself,—Tocsin, whose arrival at the Old
Bailey (never .appearing there unless specially
retained) arouses interest in the languid ushers
and door-porters, used up with constant criminal
details, but sure of some excitement when Tocsin
leads,—Tocsin is at Broadstairs, swimming and
walking with his boys during the day, and of an
evening very much interested, and not unfre-
quently affected to tears, by the Minerva-Press
novels, obtained from the little library, which he
reads aloud to his wife. Mr. Serjeant Slink,
leader at the Parliamentary Bar, whose professional life is passed in denouncing the aristocracy
of this country as stifling all freedom of political
opinion by threats or bribery, is staying with the
Duke and Duchess of Potiphar at their villa on
the Lake of Como ; and Mr. Moss of Thavies Inn,
'cutest and cleverest of criminal attorneys, is
at Venice, occupying the moments which his
valet de place allows him to have to himself
in working out the outline of the defence in a
case of gigantic fraud, the trial of which is com-

ing off next sessions, in his room at Danieli's
Hotel.

Lethargy and languor in the public offices,
where the chiefs are away on leave, and the juniors ·
left in town appear, from the medical certificates
they are sending in, to be suffering from every
kind of mortal illness, and where the "immediate
attention" promised to your communication becomes more vague and shadowy than ever; in
merchants' establishments, where the clerks, finding it impossible to get "regularly away," compromise the matter by taking lodgings at Graves-
end or in up-the-river villages, and running to
and fro daily; in large shops, where the assist-
ants bless the early-closing movement, and bound
away on Saturday afternoon with an agility which
argues well for their jumping many other things
besides counters.

George-street, Hanover-square, is much too distinguished a quarter not to suffer under the
general depression. There has not been a marriage at the church for six weeks; the rector is
away at the Lakes; and the clerk has modified his

responses, and is saving his voice until the return
of those to whom it is worth his while to address
himself.   The beadle has laid by his gorgeous
uniform, on week-days wears mufti, and on Sun-
days comes out in a kind of compromise, altern-
ately airing the hat and the coat, but never ap-
pearing in both together.   The pew-openers' un-
tipped palms are grimier than ever, the regular
congregation are absent, no strangers ask for
seats, and the dust on the pews is an inch thick.
No horsey-looking men, chewing toothpicks, and
spitting refreshingly around, garnish the portals
of Limmer's; the silver sand sprinkled over the
door-steps as usual is untrodden, save by the
pumps of the one waiter, who knows no one is
likely to come; and as weary as ever was Mariana
in her moated grange, he lounges to the door,
yawns, and lounges back, to cover his head with
his napkin for fly-diverting purposes, and seeks
refuge in sleep.   The dentist is out of town; and
the dentist's man has exchanged his striped jacket
and his black trousers for a heather suit, specially
recommended by the tailor for deer-stalking or

grouse-shooting, clad in which, he sits during the daytime in the dining-room reading *Bell's Life*, and at night, after delicately scenting himself with camphor procured from his master's drug-drawers, proceeds to some garden of public resort. The paper patterns, marked with mysterious numbers, and inscribed with the names of dukes and marquises, which hang in the shop of Stecknadel the tailor, have a thick coating of dust; for the noble customers whose fair proportions they represent have not had them in requisition for weeks past. Stecknadel is away at Boppard on the Rhine, where he has a very pretty *terre*, to which, if he could only get in his debts, he would retire, and some day become Baron Stecknadel, and live peacefully and prosperously for the rest of his life.

Equally, of course, the headless dummies in Madame Clarisse's show-rooms are stripped of the fairy-like fabrics which cover them during the season, and stand up showing all their wire anatomy, or lie about in corners, unheeded. Madame is at Dieppe, and Daisy reigns temporarily in her

stead.   The staff is very much reduced, for there
is little or nothing to do; and Daisy is enabled,
very much to Paul Derinzy's delight, to get out
much earlier and much more frequently than she
could in the season, and the walks in Kensington-
gardens occur pretty constantly, and are much
prolonged.   Daisy is glad of this too; for not
only does her liking for Paul increase, but she
knows he is very soon going away for his holiday,
"down to his people in the West," and the idea
of parting with him is not pleasant to her, and she
likes to see as much of him as possible.   Daisy
has noticed that, with the absence of the great
world from London, Paul has grown much bolder :
he walks with her without showing any of that
dreadful feeling of restraint which at one time
galled her so much, is never fearful of being
observed, and has more than once asked to be
allowed to take her to dinner, to the theatre,
or to some public gardens.   This request Daisy
has always steadily refused, and their meetings
are confined to Kensington - gardens as hereto-
fore, though she has permitted him to see her

home to the corner of her street on several occasions.

One hot dusty afternoon Daisy is looking out of the show-room window into the deserted street —deserted save by a vagabond dog, with his tongue lolling out of his mouth, who is furtively gliding about from one bit of shade to another, and hopelessly sniffing at those places where he remembers puddles used to be in the bygone time, but where, alas, there are none now—when she hears steps upon the stairs, and turning round, recognises Miss Orpington, one of their best customers. With Miss Orpington is her father, Colonel Orpington; and looking at them as they enter the room, Daisy thinks within herself that a more stylish-looking father and daughter could scarcely be found in England. Both are tall and slim and upright; both have regular features, with the same half-haughty, half-weary expression; both have small hands and feet. Miss Orpington is going to be married to a Yorkshire baronet with money. She has been staying in the same house with him in Scotland, and is on her way to a house in

Kent, where he is invited. She has stopped a day or two in London on her way through to get " some gowns and things." She is always wanting gowns and things, and spends a very large sum of money yearly.

Colonel Orpington does not very much mind how much she spends. Through his wife, who was the daughter of his family solicitor, and who died in childbirth a year after their marriage, he had a very large income, every farthing of which he carefully spent. He had nothing to do with the turf; hunted but little, and when he did, generally found other men to mount him; never joined in the afternoon rubbers at the club, and only interested himself in them to the extent of an occasional small bet; kept a good but small stud; had no permanent country place; and during the season entertained well, but neither frequently nor lavishly, and yet managed to get through eight thousand a-year.

How? Well, the Colonel had his tastes. Though turned fifty years of age, he had not run to flesh; his figure was yet trim and elegant, and

his face handsome and eminently "bred"-looking.
His hair was still jet black; and though his moustache, long, sweeping, and carefully trained, was
unmistakably grizzled, the colour rather added
to the picturesqueness of his appearance. And the
Colonel liked to be thought handsome, and elegant, and picturesque; for he was devoted to the
sex, and had but little care in life beyond how
best to please her who for the time being was the
object of his devotion.

And yet Colonel Orpington was never seen in
any suspicious *solitude à deux*, nor even in the
loose-talking, easy-going society in which he mixed
was his name ever coupled with any woman's.
Old comrades and contemporaries might be seen
lurking at the back of shady little boxes on the
pit-tier of the theatre, and addressing a presumed
form in the corner facing the stage, of which nothing could be seen but a white gleaming arm, a
fan, and an opera-glass; but when the Colonel
patronised the drama, which was very seldom, he
always went with a party among whom were his
daughter and his sister, who kept house for him.

Sons of old comrades, and other young men with whom he had a casual acquaintance, might lounge across the rails of the Row to speak to the " strange women" on horseback who were just beginning to put in an appearance there; but the Colonel, when he passed them, whether Miss Orpington were with him or not, was always looking straight before him between his horse's ears, and never showed the slightest recognition of their presence. Nor, though living in days when to love your neighbour's wife was a rule pretty generally followed, was Colonel Orpington's name ever mixed up with any of those society intrigues the ignoring of which in public, and the discussion of which in private, affords so much delight to well-bred people. Of good appearance, of perfect manners, and with a voice and address which were singularly insinuating, the Colonel might have availed himself of many *bonnes fortunes* which would not have fallen in the way of men younger and less discreet; but he purposely neglected the opportunities offered, and, while being the intimate and trusted companion of many of his friends' wives, sisters, and daughters, was the lover of none.

And yet he was devoted to the sex, and spent a great deal of money! Yes, and was very frequently absent from his family. Amongst the property which the Colonel inherited from his wife were some slate-quarries and lead-mines in South Wales, which seemed to require a vast amount of personal supervision. If he looked after the rest of his estate with equal fidelity, he must have been a pattern landlord; for he would leave town in the height of the season, or give up any pleasant engagement, when he received one of these summonses. When Miss Orpington was a child, she used to tease her father about " dose 'orrid quarry-mines;" but it was noticed that after she had put away childish things, amongst which might be enumerated innocence, she never referred to the subject. Nobody ever did palpably refer to it, though there was a good deal of sniggering about it in the Colonel's clubs, and Bobus, known as Badger Bobus from his low sporting tastes, was asked out to dinner for a fortnight on the strength of his having said that he couldn't make out how old Orpington always went into South Wales by the Great Northern Railway.

Miss Orpington languidly expresses her pleasure at seeing Daisy.

"You are so fresh, Miss Stafford, and all that kind of thing. Of course I know Madame Clarisse's taste is excellent; but I confess I like a younger person's ideas."

Daisy bows, and says nothing, but applies herself to showing her wares, which the young lady turns over and discourses upon. Colonel Orpington, standing by and caressing his grizzled moustache, says nothing also. Nothing aloud, at least; only some one standing very close might have seen him draw in his breath, and mutter behind his hand,

"Jove! Clarisse was right."

Miss Orpington is large in her notions of autumn costume, and Daisy shows her a vast number of "pretty things" which she would like to order, but is somewhat checked by the paternal presence, in itself a novelty in her negotiations with her milliner. But, deferring to the paternal presence, as to " Should she ?" and " Did he think she might ?" and receiving nothing but favourable replies, she gives her fancy scope, and makes such of the workwomen as were always retained think that the season had suddenly and capriciously recommenced.

What had induced the Colonel to accompany his daughter ? He never had done so before, and on this occasion he says nothing, never looks at the things exhibited, or the patterns after which they are to be made. What does he look at ? Miss Orpington knows, perhaps, when, following the earnest gaze of his eyes, she makes a little *moue,* and slightly shrugs her shoulders, taking no farther notice until they are in the street ; then she says :

" Do you think that girl pretty, papa ?"

The Colonel is in an abstracted state, and pauses for a minute before he replies,

" What girl, Constance ?"

" We have not seen so many that you need

ask," says Miss Orpington, with a melancholy
glance at the deserted streets; "the girl who attended to me just now, at Clarisse's."

"I was thinking of something else at the time,
and really did not notice her particularly, my
dear," says the Colonel; "but she appeared to
me to be a very respectable young person."

Miss Orpington gives her little shoulder-shrug,
and looks round curiously at her father; but he
is staring straight before him, and they walk on
without speaking farther, until just as they are
passing Limmer's, when he says, half to himself,
"That fellow will do!" and then to her,

"I want to send a message to the club, Constance. If you'll walk quietly on, I'll overtake
you in an instant.—Hi! here!"

The man to whom he calls, and who is hanging about the doorway of the hotel, is one of those
Mercuries who have now been superseded by the
Commissionnaires, but who in those days were the
principal media for good and evil communication
in the metropolis. In the season this fellow
wears a dingy red jacket like the cover of an old

Post-office Directory; but in the dead time of year he discards his gaiety of apparel, and dons a seedy long drab waistcoat with black sleeves. He crosses the road at once at the Colonel's call, and stands on the kerb, touching his broken hat, and waiting for his orders.

"Look here," says the Colonel, as soon as his daughter is out of earshot; "go up to Clarisse's —the milliner's, you know, opposite the church —ask to see the young woman who just attended to Miss Orpington, and tell her you have been sent to say she must be certain to send the things at the time promised. Take notice of her, so that you will know her again; then wait about until she comes out, follow her, see whom she speaks to and where she goes, and come to Batt's Hotel in Dover-street and ask for Colonel Orpington. You understand?"

"Right you are, Colonel!" says the man, pocketing the half-crown which the Colonel hands to him; then he touches his shabby hat again, and starts off.

"Left her walking up and down in Kensington-gardens among the trees near the keeper's
cottage, did he?" says Colonel Orpington to himself as he strikes into the Park about five o'clock,
and hurries off in the direction indicated. "Had
not spoken to any one, but seemed as if she were
waiting for somebody, eh? Plainly an assigna-
tion! So my young friend is not so innocent as
Clarisse would have me believe. What a fool she
was to think it, and what a fool I was to believe
her! However, I may as well see it through, for
the girl is marvellously pretty, and has a something about her which is extraordinarily attractive
—even to me!"

As he nears the place to which he has been
directed, he slackens his speed, and looks round
him from time to time. The first touch of autumn has fallen on the grand old trees, and occasionally some leaves come circling down noise-
lessly on to the brown turf. Away at the end of
yon vista a slight mist is rising, noticing which
the Colonel prudently buttons his coat over his
chest, and shudders slightly. Half-a-dozen chil-

dren are romping about, rolling among the leaves
that have already fallen, and shrieking with delight; but the Colonel takes no heed of them.
Just then the figures of a man and woman walking very slowly come in sight. The Colonel looks
at them for a moment, using his natty double-
eyeglass for the purpose; then stands quietly behind one of the large elm-trees watching the pair
as they pass. Her arm is through his, on which
she is leaning heavily; their faces are turned towards each other, each wearing a grave earnest
expression. As they pass the tree behind which
the Colonel stands, their faces approach, and their
lips meet for an instant; then they walk on as
before.

The Colonel drops the natty double-eyeglass
from his nose, and replaces it in his waistcoat-
pocket. As he turns to walk away, he says to
himself:

"Not a very pleasant position that! However, I've learned what I wanted to know. The
girl has a lover, as one might have expected. I
think I know the man too. To be sure! we

elected him at the Beaufort the other day—Derinzy, son of the man who put the Jew under the
pump at Hounslow. A good-looking youngster
too, and in some government office, I think. Well,
I suppose it will be the old story—youth against
cheque-book. But in this case, from the young
lady's general style, I think I should back the
latter!"

CHAPTER III.

Town was at its dreariest; the little people in Camden-town and Hackney had followed the great people in Belgravia and Tyburnia, by going away; only they went to Southend or Margate instead of Scotland or Biarritz. It was the last possible time of the year at which one would imagine festivity could take place; and yet from the aspect of No. 20 Adalbert-crescent, Navarino-road, Dalston, it was evident that festivity was intended. The general servant of the establishment had washed the upper half of her face, and hooked the lower half of her gown—an extraordinary occurrence, which meant something. The fishmonger had sent in a lobster, and half a newspaper—folded in cornucopia fashion—full of shrimps; the à-la-mode-beef house had been ransacked for the least-stony piece of cold meat which it possessed; and from the greengrocer had been obtained a perfect grove of salad and cress. Looking at these preparations, Miss Augusta Manby might well feel within herself a certain sentiment of pride, and a consciousness that Adalbert-crescent was equal to the occasion.

Miss Augusta Manby had been a workwoman at Madame Clarisse's; but she had long left that patrician establishment, and started on her own account. The name of her late employer figured under her own on the brass plate which adorned her door; and this recommendation, and her own talent in reducing bulging waists, and "fitting" generally obstinate figures, had procured for her a vast amount of patronage in the clerk-inhabited district where she had pitched her tent.

In the fulness of delight at her success, Miss Manby had taken advantage of the occasion of her birthday to summon her friends to rejoice with her at a little festive gathering, and the advent of those friends she was then awaiting.

"I think it will all do very well," she said to

herself, after surveying the preparations; "and I am sure it ought to go off nicely. I should have been afraid to ask Fanny Stafford if Bella Merton and her brother had not been coming; but she has quite West-end manners, and he is very nice-looking and very well-behaved. It's a pity I could not avoid asking Gus; but he would have been sure to have heard of it; and then if he had been left out, there would have been a pretty to-do."

A ring at the bell stopped Miss Manby's soliloquy, and she rushed to the glass to " put herself tidy," as she phrased it. There was no need for this performance in Miss Manby's case, as the glass reflected a pretty little face of the snub nose, black eyes, white teeth, and oiled-hair order, and a very pretty little figure, which the owner took care should be well, though not expensively, got up.

The arrivals were Miss Bella Merton—a young lady who officiated as clerk at Mr. Kammerer's, the photographer's in Regent-street, kept the appointment ledger, entered the number of copies

ordered, and received the money from the sitters
—and her brother, a book-keeper in Repp and
Rumfitt's drapery establishment.

" So good of you, Bella dear, to be the first!"
said Miss Manby, welcoming a tall dashing-look-
ing young woman, who darted into the room after
the half-cleansed servant had broken down in an-
nouncing " Miss Merting."—" And you too, Mr.
John ; I scarcely thought you would have taken
the trouble to come from the West-end to this
outlandish place."

Mr. John, as she called him, who was a tall
well-built young man, dressed in a black frock-
coat, waistcoat, and trousers, relieved by an alarm-
ingly vivid-blue necktie, merely bowed his acknowledgments ; but his sister, who had thrown
off a coquettish little black-silk cloak, and what
was known amongst her friends as a " duck of a
bonnet," and who was then smoothing her hair
before the one-foot-square looking-glass over the
chimney-piece, said,

" My dear Augusta, what nonsense it is ! we
who should be thankful to escape from that hot

dusty town to this—well really, this rural retreat. And as for coming early, there's nothing doing now at the west, so that one can leave when one likes."

Miss Augusta Manby then took upon herself to remark that that was one compensation for her exile from the realms of fashion. All seasons, she remarked, were the same at Dalston, where people had new clothes when the old ones were worn out, and never studied times or seasons.

"And now tell me, dear, who are coming?" said Bella Merton, while her brother John sat in the window-seat, and tried to derive a gleam of satisfaction from the inspection of the fashion-plates in *La Belle Assemblée;* "of course that dear delightful old Gus—and who else?"

"I have asked Fanny Stafford, and she has promised to come."

"No! that is fun!" said Bella Merton, laughing.

"And Mr. Burgess—"

"No! that's better still!' said Bella, laughing more heartily: "what! *our* Mr. Burgess?"

"Of course. Did he not tell you?"

"Not one single word, dear. But of course I understand why!" and the young lady relapsed into fits of merriment.

"You have all the joke to yourself at present, Bella," said John Merton, looking up from his fashion-book.

"And you won't have any of it, so far as I can see, during any part of the evening, my poor old John!" said his sister.

"I'm sorry I can't understand your West-end wit, Bella dear," said their hostess, with some asperity.

"You will see it all in a minute," said Bella, striving to compose her countenance. "Burgess has been raving-mad in love with Fanny Stafford, whom he has only seen for an instant, ever since Mr. Kammerer gave him her photograph to tint. My brother John, here, of course fell over head and ears directly he saw her; and there's another man of a different kind, with no end of money and position and all that, about whom I must say nothing. So much for Fanny Stafford. But what's to become of you and me, Augusta? There's nobody left for us but old Gus."

"What's that you are saying about old Gus?" said a fat jolly voice, belonging to a fat jolly man, of about forty years of age, who entered the room at the moment.

This was Augustus Manby, the hostess's brother, a tea-taster attached to an establishment in Mincing-lane—a convivial soul, and a thorough vulgarian.

"Saying!" said Bella Merton, whose two hands he was wringing, after having given his sister a smacking kiss; "that we should have no one but you to flirt with, all the other men would be absorbed by Fanny Stafford."

"Well, they are welcome so far as I am concerned," said plain-spoken Gus. "She's a nice girl, Fanny; but I don't like them red, and I do like more of them; and that's the fact."

"Hush! do be quiet," said his sister, as the bell sounded again; and the next minute Fanny Stothard entered the room.

She looked so lovely, that Gus almost audibly

recalled his opinion. The exercise had given a colour to her cheeks and a brilliancy to her eyes. Her dress fitted her to perfection, and there was an indefinable something about her which stamped her superiority to those among whom she then was. She was warmly welcomed by all, and had scarcely gone through their greetings when Mr. Burgess joined, and completed the little party.

Mr. Burgess was a small consumptive-looking young man, principally remarkable for the length of his hair and the smallness of his cravat. Believing in his destiny as an "arteeste," he had originally entered as a student at the Royal Academy; but after severe objurgations from the authorities there, had subsided into colouring pictures for the photographers, by which he realised a decent income. He entered the room with a bound suggestive of hope and joy; but on seeing Fanny he sighed deeply, and abandoned himself to misery.

Then they all bustled about, and the cloth was laid, and the provisions produced, and the half-cleansed servant appeared periodically, staggering under large pewter vessels containing malt liquor; and the gentlemen pressed the ladies to eat and to drink; and the ladies would not be persuaded without a great deal of pressing on the gentlemen's part; and so the meal was gone through with much giggling and laughter, but without any regular talk.

That began when the hostess had fetched from a cupboard, where they were imbedded in layers of brown-paper patterns and bygone fashion-books, and watched over by an armless papier-maché idol, two bottles of spirits; and when the gentlemen had brewed themselves mighty jorums of grog, and helped the ladies to delicate wine-glasses of the same beverage. And thus it commenced:

"Things must be dull with you now at Clarisse's, Fanny dear?" said the hostess.

"Dull!" said Fanny; "I never knew anything like it. I don't mean written orders from the country, of course; but we only had one customer in our place the whole of last week."

"What will you bet me, Fanny," said Bella

Merton, "that I don't tell you that customer's name?"

"Why, how can you possibly know it? She—"

"I don't speak of a she! I mean a he," said Bella, laughing.

"Hes ain't milliners' customers," said Mr. Burgess, with a titter.

"Ain't they?" said John Merton, with a savage expression on his good-looking face; "but they are sometimes, worse luck!"

"My customer, at all events, was a lady," said Fanny, rather disapproving of this turn of the conversation.

"Yes; but she was accompanied by a gentleman," said Bella, still laughing; "and, as John says, gentlemen have no right in milliners' show-rooms."

"I suppose that even Mr. John Merton would not object to a father's accompanying his daughter to a milliner's show-room?" said Fanny, beginning to be piqued.

"Mr. John Merton merely spoke generally, Miss Stafford," said John, with a bow. "He

would not have taken the liberty to apply his observation to any particular case."

"This is perfectly delicious!" cried Bella
Merton, clapping her hands. "I knew I should
soon set you all by the ears. But we have wandered from my original proposition. Can I, or
can I not, tell you the name of the gentleman
who came with his daughter, as you say, to your
place last week?"

"I daresay you can," said Fanny Stothard,
"though how you gained your information it
would be impossible for me to say."

"Don't tell her, Miss Stafford," said John
Merton; "don't help her in the least degree.
It's scarcely a fair subject of conversation; at
least, it's one which I'm sure has no interest for
me."

"Was he a nice cross old dear?" said his
sister; "and didn't he like to hear about the fine
gentlemen that admired Fanny?"

John Merton looked so black at this remark,
that Mr. Burgess thought it best to cut into the
conversation. So he said:

" But you haven't yet told us the name of the gentleman, Miss Merton."

" Haven't I?" said Bella; " well, I'll be as good as my word. Colonel Orpington. Am I right, Fanny?"

" I daresay you are. Miss Orpington's father came with her. What his title may be, I haven't the least idea."

" But he knows what your title is, dear, and accords it to you quite publicly."

" And what title does he give Miss Stafford, pray?" asked John Merton angrily.

" That of the prettiest girl in London!"

" I never heard a swell go so near the truth," growled John, half pleased and half annoyed.

" Don't you think it is almost time for you to speak a little more plainly, Bella?" asked Fanny. " How do you know this Colonel Orpington, and what has he been saying about me?"

" *This* Colonel Orpington, indeed!" cried Miss Merton. " My dear, *this* Colonel Orpington is simply one of the best men of the day, extremely rich, and—well, you know—one of those nice fel-

lows who are liked by everybody. He came into
our place the other day, and when I looked up
from my desk in the front room, where I was
writing a private letter—for I had nothing else to
do—I saw him; and I thought to myself, ' I know
you, Colonel Orpington! I've seen you about
often. So you've come for a sitting, have you?
Won't Mr. Kammerer be wild to think you should
have come when he was out of town !' However,
he came straight towards me ; and he took off his
hat, like a gentleman as he is, and he said,
' There is a portrait in a frame outside the door
which strikes me as a wonderful example of pho-
tography, of which I am a connoisseur.' I knew
what he meant at once, bless you ; but I said,
' You mean the gentleman in the skull-cap and
the long beard—Professor Gilks ?' He muttered
something about Professor Gilks—I daren't say
what—but then said no ; he meant the coloured
female head—was it for sale ? I told him I could
not answer him without referring to Mr. Kammerer, who was at Ramsgate. The Colonel begged
me to telegraph to him, and he would call next

day. He did call next day, took the photograph, and paid twenty guineas for it, which was a good thing for Mr. Kammerer."

"Very likely," burst in John Merton; "but a bad thing for art, and decency, and—"

"Don't distress yourself, John! Very likely it was all you say; but, you see, Mr. Kammerer is not here for you to pitch into, and Fanny couldn't help her portrait being bought by an admirer. O, he was an admirer, Fanny; for when I tied it up for him, he said out, 'It's lovely, but it doesn't do justice to the original.' And when I asked him, did he know the original, he said he thought he had had that honour. And so it's no good your bursting into virtuous indignation."

Her brother shrugged his shoulders and was silent; but Fanny Stothard said:

"Don't you think this joke has gone far enough? Augusta and Mr. Burgess here are sitting in wild astonishment, as well they may be. Let us change the conversation for the few minutes before we break up."

Late that night Fanny Stothard sat on the
side of her bed in her room in South Molton-
street, her hands clasped behind her head, her
body gently swaying to and fro as she pondered
over all she had heard that evening. On the
table lay a letter from Paul Derinzy. It was the
second she had had, and he had not been away
from London five days. The first she had torn
at eagerly and devoured its contents at once; this
lay unopened.

"Very rich, that woman said," she muttered,
"and a great man in his way. Fancy his buying
the portrait, and after only seeing me once! That
was very nice of him. Not in the least old-look-
ing, and everybody likes him, Bella said. What
a funny thing his recognising that photograph,
and— How horrible the journey home was to-
night, and what detestable people in the omnibus!
—such pushing and tramping on one's feet, and
—I had no idea of that! I thought he looked
hard at me once or twice, but I never imagined
that he took any particular notice. Colonel Orpington! I shall look out his name in the *Court*

Guide to-morrow, when I get to George-street, and see all about him. Had the honour of knowing me, he told Bella Merton! Ugh! how sick I am of this room, and how wearied of this life! Ah, well, Paul's letter will keep till to-morrow; I'm sure I know what it's about. That was really very nice about the portrait! I wonder when Colonel Orpington will come back to town."

Then she frowned a little as she said, "What could have made that young man, Bella's brother, so disagreeable about all that? He couldn't possibly—and yet I don't know. He looked so earnestly at me, and spoke so strongly about that business of the portrait, that I have half an idea he resented it on my behalf. What impertinence! And yet he meant merely to show his regard for me. How dreadfully in earnest he seemed! And Paul too! I shall have a difficulty in managing them all, I see that clearly."

CHAPTER IV.

PAUL AT HOME.

It does not matter much to George Wainwright whether London is empty or full. His books, his work, and his healthful play go on just the same in winter and summer, in spring and autumn. He only knows it is the season by the fact of seeing more people in the streets, more horses and carriages in the Park across which he strides to his home; and when other men go away on leave, he remains at the office without the least desire to change the regular habits of his life. He has a splendid constitution, perfectly sound, and unimpaired by excess of any description; can do any amount of work without its having any influence on him; and never had need to go away " on medical certificate," as is the case with so many of his brethren at the Stannaries Office.

There is a decidedly autumnal touch in the
air as it plays round George Wainwright, striding
across the Park this October morning. There is
sunshine, but it is thin and veneered, and very
unlike the glorious summer article; looks as if it
had lost strength in its struggle with the fog
which preceded it, and as though it would make
but a poor fight against the mist which would
come creeping up early in the afternoon. But
few leaves remain on the trees, and they are yel-
low and veinous, and swirl dismally round and
round in their descent to the moist earth, where
their already fallen comrades are being swept into
heaps, and pressed down into barrows, and wheeled
away by the gardeners. The ordinarily calm
waters of the Serpentine are lashed into minia-
ture waves, and the pleasure-boats have vanished
from its surface, as have the carriages from the
Drive and the horses from the Row. Only one
solitary equestrian stands out like a speck in the
distance; for it is Long Vacation still, and the
judges and the barristers, those unvarying early
riders and constant examples of the apparently

insurmountable difficulty of combining legal lore
with graceful equitation, have not yet returned to
town.

Ten o'clock strikes from the Horse-Guards
clock as George walks under the archway, and
makes his way across to the little back street
where the Stannaries Office is situated. Always
punctual, he is more particular than ever just
now, for all the others of any standing are away;
and George was perfectly aware, from long experience, that if some one responsible was not there
to look after the junior clerks, those young gentlemen would not come at all. As it was, he
finds himself the first arrival, and has changed
his coat and rung for his letters—for even the
messengers get lax and careless at this time of
year—when the door opens and Mr. Dunlop enters, bringing with him a very strong flavour of
fresh tobacco, and not stopping short in the po-
pular melody which he is humming to say good-
day until he has arrived at the end of the verse.

" ' And he cut his throat with a pane of glass,
and stabbed his donkey ar-ter !' " sings Mr. Dun-

lop, very much prolonging the last note. " That's
what I call an impressive ending to a tragic bal-
lad!—Good-morning, Mr. Wainwright! I'm glad
to see you here in good time for once, sir, at all
events."

" Billy, Billy, if you were here a little earlier
yourself, you wouldn't be pitched into so constantly."

" Perhaps not, sir, though ' pitched into' is
scarcely a phrase to apply to a gentleman in her
Majesty's Civil Service. However, my position is
humble, and I must demean myself accordingly.
I am a norphan, sir, a norphan, and have no
swell parents to stay with in the country like Mr.
Derinzy, whose remarkably illegible and insigni-
ficant handwriting I recognise on this letter which
Hicks has brought in for you."

" Paul's hand, by Jove!" says George, " and
this other one is Courtney's, the chief's."

George opens the smaller letter, and emits a
short whistle as he glances through its contents.
The whistle and the expression of George's face
are not lost upon Billy Dunlop, who says :

"Dear old person going to make it three months' leave, this year, instead of two? or perhaps not coming back at all, but sends address where his salary will find him?"

"On the contrary, he's coming back at once; he will be on duty to-morrow."

"By Jove! and he's not been away six weeks yet. The poet was right, sir. 'He stabbed his donkey arter!' There was nothing else left for him to do."

"But," says George, laughing, "he says he thinks he shall go away to Brighton in November, and advises me, if I want any leave, to take it now, that I may be back when he goes."

"What an inexpressible old ruffian! What does he say about my leave?"

"Not a word. What could he say, Billy? You've had all your leave ages ago."

Mr. Dunlop, who has retired into the sanctuary behind the washing-screen, makes a rapid reappearance at these words, and says hurriedly:

"I thought so. I thought that that pleasant month of March would be the only portion of the year allotted to me for recreation. March, by George! Why, Ettrick, Teviotdale, and all the rest of them put together, are not worth speaking about. It seems a year ago. I can only recollect it because it was so beastly cold I was obliged to spend nearly all the time in bed. That's a nice way for a man to enjoy his holiday! While you fellows are cutting about, and— Hollo! what's the matter with G. W.? He looks as if he were rapidly preparing himself for his father's asylum. Some bad news from P. D., I suppose."

These last remarks of Mr. Dunlop's are based upon his observation of George Wainwright's face, the expression of which is set and serious.

" Hold on with your chaff for a minute, Billy," he says, looking up. " Paul is writing on business, and I want just to get hold of it as I go along."

So Mr. Dunlop thinks he will do a little official work; and having selected a sheet of foolscap with " Office of H.M. Stannaries" lithographed on it, fills-in the date in a very bold and flowing hand (the gentlemen of the Stannaries Office al-

ways boasted that they were not " mere clerks,"
and that their penmanship " didn't matter"), then
takes out his penknife, and begins adjusting the
toilet of his nails.

Meanwhile George Wainwright plods his way
with difficulty through Paul's letter where the
writing is so small and the lines so close together, and his brow becomes more contracted and
his face more set and stern as he proceeds.   This
is what he reads :

" *The Tower, Beachborough.*

" DEAR OLD MAN,—I have so much writing at
that confounded shop—don't grin, now ; I can see
your cynical old under - lip shooting - out at the
statement—that I thought I'd give my pen a
holiday as well as myself; and indeed I should
not favour you with a sight of that ' bowld fist'
which so disgusts that old beast Branwhite—saw
his name in the *Post* as having been present at
the Inverness gathering, hanging on to swells as
usual—if there had not been absolute occasion.

"By Jove ! what a tremendously long sentence
that is !   Rather broken-backed and weak in the

knees too, eh ? Don't seem to hang well together ? Rather a ' solution of continuity,' as they
call it, isn't there ? Never mind, you'll understand what I mean. You see, my dear old George,
I don't know whether it is because I'm bored by
being in the country—and a fellow who is accustomed to town life must necessarily hate everything else, and find it all horribly slow and dreary
—but the fact is, that instead of my leave doing
me good, and setting me up, and all that kind
of thing, I find myself utterly depressed and
wretched, and nothing like half so well or so jolly
as when I came down here.

"I thought I should go out boating and swimming and riding, and generally larking; and instead of that I find myself sitting grizzling over
my pipe, and wondering what on earth I'm to do
until evening, and how I shall get through the
time after dark until I can go to bed.

"You would go blazing away at your old
books, or your writing, or your music; but I'm
not in that line, old boy. I haven't got what
people call ' resources'—in any way, by Jove ! tin,

or anything else. I want to be amused, and I don't get it here, and that's all about it.

"You see, the truth is—and what's the good of having a fellow for your pal if you can't speak the truth to him, and what people in the play call 'unbosom yourself,' and so on?—the truth is, our household here is most infernally dull. I hadn't seen any of them for so long, that they all came upon me like novelties; and they're so deuced original, that they would be most interesting studies, if they did not happen to be one's own people, don't you see, and that takes all the humour out of the performance. There's my governor, for instance, is the most wonderful party! If he were anybody else's governor, he'd be quite good fun enough for me to render the place sufficiently agreeable. I don't think I should want any greater amusement than seeing him go yawning about the house and through the village, bored out of his life, and wishing everything at the devil. He seemed to pluck up a bit when I first came down, and wanted to know all the news about town, and talked about this fellow and that

fellow—I knew the names well enough, and had
met a good many of the people; but when we
came to compare notes, I found that the governor
was inquiring about the fathers of the fellows I
knew—fellows with the same names, you understand; and when I explained this to him, and
told him that most of his pals were dead or gone
under, don't you know, and that their sons
reigned in their stead, he cut up rather rough,
and said he didn't know what the world was coming to, and that young men weren't half as well
brought-up nowadays as they were in his time.
Funny idea that, wasn't it? As though we could
help these old swells going under! Fact is—I
don't like to confess it, and would not to anybody
but you, George—but since the governor has got
off the main line of life they have shunted him
into the siding for fogeydom, and there's not much
chance of his coming out again.

"I find a great change in my mother too.
I've spoken to you so often about all these domes-
ticities, that I don't mind gossiping to you now.
It's an immense relief to me. I feel if I had not

some one to confide in, I should blow up. Well, you know, my mother was always the best man in our household, and managed everything according to her own will; but then she had a certain tact and *savoir-faire*, a way of ruling us all that no one could find fault with; and though we grumbled inwardly, we never took each other into confidence, or combined against the despotism. I find that's all altered now. Either she has lost tact, or we have lost patience—a little of both, perhaps; but, at all events, her attempts at rule and dictation are very palpable and very pronounced, and our ripeness for revolt is no longer concealed. In point of fact, the one thing which the governor and I have in common is our impatience of the female thrall, and if ever we combine it will be to pass the Salic law.

"And *apropos* of that—rather neatly expressed, I find that is—there is another female pretender to power — my cousin Annette; you have heard me speak of her as a ward of my people's, and resident with them. She has grown into a fine young woman, though her manners are de-

cidedly odd. I suppose this is country breeding:
said as much to the governor, who made a very
odd face and changed the subject. Whether he
thought it the height of impudence in me to suppose that any one who had had the advantage of
studying him daily could have country manners,
or whether there was any other reason, I don't
know.

"One thing there can be no doubt of, and
that is, that I am always being thrown *tête-à-tête*
with this young woman, principally, as I imagine,
by my mother's connivance. This might have
been amusing under other circumstances, for, as
I said before, she is remarkably personable and
nice—not in my line, but still a very fine young
woman; but, situated as I am, I do not avail myself in the slightest degree of the opportunities
offered.

"Nor, I am bound to say, does Annette. She
sits silent, and sometimes actually sullen. She
is a most extraordinary girl, George; I can't make
her out a bit. Sometimes she won't speak for
hours, sometimes won't even come down amongst

us, and— There is something deuced odd in all
this! I wish I had your clear old head here to
scrutinise matters with me, and help me in form-
ing a judgment on them.

"You know what I refer to just above about
' under other circumstances'? Certain interview
in Kensington-gardens with certain party that you
happened to witness. Don't you recollect? O
Lord, George, if you knew what an utterly gone
coon I am in that quarter, you would pity me.
No, you wouldn't! What's the use of talking to
such a dried-up old file as you about such things?
I don't believe you were ever in love in your life,
ever felt the smallest twinge of what those stupid
fools the poets call the ' gentle passion.' Gentle,
by Jove! it's anything but gentle with me—up-
sets me frightfully, takes away all my sleep, and
worries me out of my life. I swear to you, that
now I am separated from her I don't know how to
live without her, and wonder how I ever got on
before I knew her. When I think I'm far away
from everybody, on the cliffs or down by the sea,
I find myself holloing out aloud, and stamping

my foot, for sheer rage at the thought that so
much more time must go by before I can see her
again. I told you it was a strong case, George,
when you spoke to me about it; but I had no
idea then that it was so strong as it is, or that
my happiness was half so much bound up in
her."

There was a space here, and the conclusion of
the letter, from the appearance of the ink, had
evidently been written at a different time.

"I left off there, George, thinking I might
have something else to say to you later; and so
I have, but of a very different kind from what I
imagined.

"I have had a tremendous scene with my
mother. She has given up hinting, and spoken
out plainly at last. It appears that her whole
soul is set upon my marrying my cousin Annette.
This is the whole and sole reason of their living
out of town, and of the poor governor being expa-
triated from the Pall-Mall pavement and the gos-

sip he loves so well. It appears that Annette is an heiress—in rather a large way too, will have no end of money—and that my poor dear mother, determined to secure her for me, has been hiding down here in this horrible seclusion, in order that the girl may form no 'detrimental' acquaintance of youths who might be likely to cut me out! Not very flattering to me, is it? But still it was well meant, poor soul!

"Now, you know, George, this won't do at all. If I entered into this plan for a moment, I should have to give up that other little affair at once; *and nothing earthly would make me do that!* Besides, I do not care for Annette; and as to her money, that would be deuced little good to me, if— However, one goes with the other, so we needn't say any more about it.

"Of course, I fought off at once—pleaded Annette's bad state of health—she is ill, often keeps her room, and has to have a nurse entirely given up to her—said we were both very young, and asked for time—but all no good. My mother was very strong on the subject; and the governor, who sees a chance of his jailership being put an end to, and of his getting back to haunts of civilisation, backed her up with all his might, which is not much, poor old boy!

"So all I could do was to say that I never did anything without your advice, and to suggest that you should be asked down here at once. My mother wouldn't have it at first, until I said she feared you were a gay young dog who would make running with Annette to my detriment; and then I told her what a quiet, solemn, old-fashioned old touch you really were, and then she consented. So, dear old man, you're booked and in for it. I really do want your counsel awfully, though I only thought of making you a scapegoat when I first suggested your visit. But now I am looking forward to it with the greatest anxiety from day to day. Come at once. You can easily arrange about your leave,—come, and help me in this fix. *But recollect, don't attempt to break off the acquaintance between me and that young lady, for that would be utterly useless!* God bless you. Come at once.—Yours ever,   P. D."

George Wainwright reads this letter through twice attentively, and the frown deepens on his forehead. Then he folds it up, and places it in his breast-pocket, and remains for ten minutes, slowly stroking his beard with his hand, and pondering the while. Then he looks up, and says,

"Billy, I'm thinking of taking the chief's advice, and going for a little leave."

"O, certainly," says Mr. Dunlop; "don't mind me, I beg. Leave the whole work of the department on my shoulders, pray. You'll find I'm equal to the occasion, sir; and perhaps in some future time, when I have 'made by force my merit known'—when the Right Honourable William Dunlop is First Lord of the Treasury, has clutched the golden keys, and shaped the whisper of the Throne into saying in the ear of the Chancellor of the Exchequer, 'Put W. D. on the pension-list for ten thou.'—I may thank you for having given me the opportunity of distinguishing myself!"

CHAPTER V.

"WELL, George, old man, how are you? No need to ask, though. You're looking as fresh as a daisy, and that after a couple of hundred miles of rail, a long drive in a dog-cart, and a family dinner with people who were strangers to you! And after all that, you're up and out by nine o'clock. I told my people you were the most wonderful fellow in the world, and now I think they'd believe it."

"I haven't done anything yet to assert any claim to such a character, at all events, Paul. I'm always an early riser, and most certainly I wasn't going to loaf away a splendid morning like this between the sheets. Where are the ladies and the Captain?"

"My mother is generally occupied with

domestic matters in the morning, and Annette never shows till later in the day. If the governor had had his will, he would have liked to be with us now. He was immensely fetched by you last night, and jabbered away as I have not heard him for years. But a little of the governor goes a long way; and I told him we had business to talk over this morning; so he's off on his own hook somewhere, poor old boy."

"I don't think you appreciate your father quite sufficiently, Master Paul. He made himself remarkably agreeable last night; and there was a kind of *Pelham* and *Tremaine* flavour about his conversation which was particularly refreshing in this back-slapping, slangy age."

"And Annette—what did you think of her?"

"I was very much struck with her appearance. I'm not much of a judge in such matters, but surely she is very pretty?"

"Ya-as," said Paul with a half-conquering air, caressing his moustache; "ya-as, she is pretty. What did you think of her — of her altogether, you know?"

"I thought her manner very charming. A little timid and nervous, as was natural on being introduced to a stranger. Well, even more than timid : a little weary, as though scarcely recovered from some illness or excitement."

"Ah, that was her illness. She had a bout of it the very day I sent off my letter to you."

"Well, she gave me that idea. But what on earth did you mean, young fellow, by telling me in that letter that your cousin was dull and *distraite?* I never saw any one more interested or more interesting ; and what she said about Wordsworth's sonnets and his poem of 'Ruth' was really admirably thought out and excellently put."

"Exactly. And yet you demur at my calling you the most wonderful fellow in the world ! Why, my dear old George, you are the first person in all our experience of her that has ever yet made Annette talk."

"Perhaps because I am the first person who has listened to her."

"Not at all ! We've all of us tried it. The

governor's not much, to be sure, and those who
don't care to hear perpetually about the Tambu-
rini row, and D'Orsay, and Gore House, and
'glorious Jack Reeve at the Adelphi, sir!' and
those kind of interesting anecdotes, soon get
bored. And I'm not much, and not often here.
But my mother, as you'll soon find out, is a
clever woman, capital talker, and all that; and so
far as I can learn, Miss Netty has hitherto utterly
refused to be interested and amused even by that
most fascinating of men to the sex, your father."

"My father! Why, where did he ever see
Miss Derinzy?"

"Here, in this very house. Ay, you may
well look astonished! It appears that my people
knew your father in early years, before he took up
his present specialty, and that he attended my
mother, who has never had anything like decent
health. She grew so accustomed to him that she
would never see any one else; and Dr. Wainwright
has been good enough, since they have been here,
to come down two or three times a-year, and look
after her."

" And he has seen Miss Derinzy ?"

" O yes; unprofessionally, of course—at dinner, and that kind of thing—and, as I understand, has gone in to make himself very agreeable to Annette, but has never succeeded. On the contrary."

" On the contrary ?"

" Well, they tell me that she has always snubbed him tremendously; and that must have been a frightful blow to such a society swell as your governor, George—diner-out, and *raconteur*, and all that kind of thing. Fact of the matter is, she has a deuced bad provincial style about her."

" Upon my honour I can't see it, can't allow it, even though, as you say, she did snub my father."

" Of course not, you old muff! Antony, no doubt, thought Cleopatra's manners charming; though the ' dull cold-blooded Cæsar' who wouldn't be hooked in, and the other gents whom Antony cut out, had not a good word for her. However, look here; this scheme won't do at all. Don't you see that ?"

" What scheme ?"

"Now, 'pon my word, I call this nice! I fire guns for help, ring an alarm-bell for aid, and when the aid comes I have to explain my case! Don't you recollect what I told you about my mother's plan for my marrying Annette?"

"O—yes," said George Wainwright slowly, "I recollect now."

"That's deuced kind of you. So, you must see it would never do."

"It would not do?"

"No, of course it wouldn't! What a fellow you are, George!" said Paul, almost testily. "The girl does not suit me in the smallest degree, and —and there's another one that does."

"Ah, I had forgotten about that."

"My good fellow, you seem to have left your wits behind you at the office for Billy Dunlop to take care of. What the deuce are you mooning about?"

"Nothing; I was only a little confused for the moment. And you are still over head and ears in that quarter, my poor Paul?"

"By Jove, you may well say that!"

"You correspond, of course, during your absence?"

"I've heard from her once or twice."

"And you carry the letters there," touching his friend's breast-pocket. "Ah, I heard a responsive crackling of paper, my poor old Paul."

"O, it's all deuced fine for you to talk about 'my poor old Paul,' and all that, but you don't know the party, or even you would be warmed into something like life!"

"Hem!" growled Wainwright, "I don't know about that; though, as you say, I am a little more exacting in my requirements than you. Does she spell Paul with a 'w,' or with a little 'p'?"

"She spells and writes like a lady as she is. What an ass I am to get into a rage! Look here, George, I can't stand this much longer. I must get back to her. It's no good my fooling my time away down here. My mother has brought me down to propose for Annette, and I shall have to tell her perfectly plainly that it can't be done."

"That's why you sent for me," said George

Wainwright; "to tell me that you had fully made up your mind in the matter on which you brought me down here to consult me, eh?"

"No, not at all. I wanted to consult you, my dear old man, my best and dearest of old boys; but, you see, the scenes have shifted a little since I wrote. I've seen more of Annette, and seen more plainly that she does not like me, and I don't care for her; and I've had a letter from town which makes me think that the sooner I'm back with Daisy, the better."

"With Daisy? that's her name, is it?"

"That's her pet name with me, and—What, mooning again, eh?"

"No, I wasn't. I was merely thinking about— Who was that elderly woman who came to the drawing-room door last night and told Miss Derinzy it was bed-time?"

"O, that was Annette's servant, who is specially devoted to her—Mrs. Stothard."

"Mrs. Stothard—Miss Derinzy's maid?"

"Well, maid, and nurse, and general attendant. Poor Annette, as I wrote you, is very delicate, and requires constant watching. I should not wonder if the excitement of last night and all your insinuating charming talk, you old rascal, were to have a bad effect, and make her lay up."

"Poor young lady, I sincerely hope not.— When did you say my father was here last?"

"I *didn't* say any time; but I believe a few weeks ago. Now let us take a turn, and try and find the governor."

"By all means. I—I suppose Miss Derinzy is not down yet?"

"Villain! you would add to the mischief you caused last night. No. Down! no; not likely to be for hours! Come."

About the time that this conversation was going on in the little breakfast-room, Mrs. Stothard might have been seen leaving the suite of apartments which she and her young mistress occupied, all the doors of which she carefully closed behind her, and making her way to Mrs. Derinzy's room. Arrived there, she gave a short knock—by no means a humble petitioning rap,

but a sort of knock which said, "I only do this kind
of thing because I am obliged" — and, following
close on the sound of her knuckles, entered.

As Mrs. Stothard had previously noticed—for
nothing escaped her—Mrs. Derinzy for the last
few days had been very much "out o' sorts," in
the language of the villagers. Those humble
souls anticipated the immediate advent of another
attack, and Mrs. Powler had even suggested to
Dr. Barton that the "man in Lunnon," as she
called Dr. Wainwright, should be sent for. But
when the little village medico presented himself
at the Tower with the view of making a few preliminary inquiries, he only saw Mrs. Stothard,
who told him, with an amount of grimness and
acidity unusual even in her, that his services were
not required.

The fact was, that Mrs. Derinzy, though to a
certain extent a strong-minded woman, had confined herself for many years to diplomacy; and
while plotting and scheming, had forgotten the
actual art of war as practised by her in early days.
Now, when the time had arrived for her to descend

again into the arena, her courage failed her. It was now that Paul should be induced—forced, if necessary—to take up that position to the preparation of which for him the best years of his mother's life had been devoted, and at this very moment Mrs. Derinzy felt herself unequal to the task. The fact is, she had been winding herself up for the struggle, and was now rapidly running down before it commenced, although—perhaps because —she had her suspicions as to the result.

"How do you find yourself this morning?" asked Mrs. Stothard in a loud unsympathetic voice.

"Not at all well, Martha. You might guess that from finding me still in my room at this time; but the fact is, I had scarcely the energy to get up this morning."

"Tired out by the wild dissipation of having a fresh face to look at, a fresh tongue to listen to, last night, I suppose."

"You mean Mr. Wainwright? He certainly is a most agreeable man."

"You are not the only person this morning

suffering from his charms," said Mrs. Stothard, with a sniff of depreciation as she pronounced the last words.

" What do you mean? How is Annette? What kind of a night did she have ?"

" Bad enough. O no, nothing violent, but bad enough for all that. I don't think I ever saw her so excited, so pleasantly excited, before. I could not persuade her to go to bed ; and she coaxed me to let her sit up while she talked to me of your visitor. He was so handsome, so charming, so intelligent, she had never seen any one like him."

" He made himself very agreeable," said Mrs. Derinzy shortly. She was alarmed at the account of these raptures on Annette's part, which boded no good to her favourite project.

" If she were a responsible being, I should say she was in love," said Mrs. Stothard. " Not that any one is responsible under those circumstances," she added : a dim remembrance of a cathedral yard, a pile of illuminated drawings, and a cornet in the cavalry, seen through a long vista of intervening years, gave her voice a flat and hollow sound.

"In love! stuff! She sees so few new faces that she's amused for the time, that's all. She will have forgotten the man by this morning."

"She *hasn't* forgotten him, though you do say 'stuff!' She had a very restless night, tossing and talking in her sleep and laughing to herself. And this morning, directly she woke, she asked me if George Wainwright was still here; and when I told her yes, laughed and kissed my cheek, and fell asleep again quite satisfied."

"*George* Wainwright, eh?" said Mrs. Derinzy. "She has lost no time in picking up his name."

"She loses no time in picking up anything that interests her. And this Mr. George Wainwright is clever, you say?"

"Very clever, so Paul says; and so he seems."

"And he has come down here on a visit, just to see Mr. Paul?"

"Exactly. Mr. Paul thinks there is nobody like him, and consults him in everything."

"And yet, knowing this," said Mrs. Stothard,

drawing nearer and dropping her voice, " you have this man here, and don't seem to see any danger in his coming."

" What do you mean, Martha ? I don't comprehend you," said Mrs. Derinzy, showing in her pallid cheeks and wandering hands how she had been taken aback by the suddenness of the question.

" O yes, you understand me perfectly, and as you have only chosen to give me half-confidences, I can't speak any plainer. But this I will say, that if you still wish to throw dust in your son's eyes as regards what is the matter with Annette, you have acted with extraordinary folly in permitting this man to come down here. He is no shallow flimsy youth like Mr. Paul—you will excuse my speaking out ; it is necessary in such matters—but a clever, shrewd, long-headed man of the world, and one, above all, who is constantly brought into contact with cases such as Annette's. He will see what is the matter with her in the course of the next interview they have, even if he has not discovered it at once, or at all events the first time she has an attack, and—he will tell his friend."

"They must be kept apart; he must not see her any more."

"Pshaw! that would excite suspicion—his, Paul's, every one's. No; we must think it out quietly, and see what can be done for the best. Meantime, Annette's state is greatly in our favour. She is wonderfully good-tempered and docile, and if she does not get too much excited, we may yet pass it off all well."

"Let her console herself with that idea," said Mrs. Stothard, when she found herself alone in her own room, "if she is weak enough to find consolation in it. Nothing will hide the truth from this man. I saw that in the mere momentary glance I had of him last night. He will detect Annette's madness, and will tax his father with the knowledge of it; and the Doctor, hard though he is, won't be able to deceive his son. And then up blows our fine Derinzy castle into the air! Won't it blow up without that? Wait

a minute, and let us just see how matters stand—
in regard to *my* plans and *my* future, I mean, not
theirs.

"Paul is still madly in love with Fanny.
Since he has been here, he has had two letters
from her, addressed to him at the Lion, under
his assumed name of 'Douglas.' I saw them
when they fell from his pocket, as he changed
his coat in the hall the other day. So far, so
good. Then — this man Wainwright finds out
that Annette is mad, and tells Paul. Of course
the young fellow declares off at once, only too
glad to do so, and Mrs. Derinzy's hopes of the
marriage are at an end.

"Would Paul marry Fanny then? If left to
himself he would; but Wainwright, who they say
has such immense influence over him, would never
permit it; would persuade him that he was dis-
gracing himself, talk about unequal alliances, and
all that.

"A dangerous man to have for an enemy!
What is to be done? How is he to be won over?
Suppose—suppose he were to take a fancy to the

girl himself, mad as she is—such things have been, and she is certainly fascinated with him —and I were to prove their friend! How would that work out? I think something might be made of it."

CHAPTER VI.

THE COLONEL'S CORRESPONDENT.

THE pleasant house in Kent at which Colonel Orpington and his daughter are staying is filled with agreeable company. Not merely young men who are out shooting all day in the thick steaming coverts well preserved with pheasants; not merely young women who are in the habit of carrying on perpetual flirtation with the afore-named young men in language intelligible to themselves alone, who look upon the Colonel as rather a fogey, and who, as he confesses himself, bore him immensely, and are very much deteriorated from the youth of his time; but several people of his own age—club-haunting men who began life when he did, and have pursued it much after the same fashion; and ladies who take interest in all the talk and scandal and reminiscences of bygone years.

The house is situated at such a little distance from town—some sixty miles or so—that it is traversed in very little more than an hour by the express train, which (the owner of the house is a director of the railway) can be always stopped by signal at the very small station nearest to it; so that the company is constantly changing, and receiving fresh accessions, the coming guests being welcomed, and the parting guests being speeded, after the ordinary recipe.

But throughout the changes, Colonel Orpington and his daughter are among the company who stay on; both of them are voted excellent company, for the nights are beginning to grow long now, and the dinner-hour has been fixed at seven instead of eight; and there is a great talk of and preparation for certain amateur theatricals, of which the Colonel, who is an old hand at such matters, is stage-manager and principal director, and in which Miss Orpington is to take a leading part. Much astonishment has been privately exhibited by certain of the assembled people that that restlessness which generally characterised "old O.," as he was familiarly termed amongst them, seemed to have abated during his visit to Harble-down Hall; more especially has a calm come over those horribly troublesome slate-quarries and lead-mines in South Wales, which usually took the Colonel so frequently away from his daughter and his friends. The matter is discussed in the smoking-room late at night, long after the well-preserved Colonel has retired to his rest; and Badger Bobus, who is come down to stay at Harbledown on the first breath of there being any possibility of cub-hunting, thinks that he ought to keep up the reputation which he acquired by his famous saying on the subject; but the Muse is unpropitious, and all that Bobus can find to remark is, that "it is deuced extraordinary."

The long interval which has now elapsed since her father found it necessary to relieve her of his presence does not seem to have had much effect upon Miss Orpington. Truth to tell, whether her revered parent is or is not with her has now be-

come a matter of very small moment with that
lady; and when her hostess congratulates herself
in supposing that her house must indeed be attractive when that dear Colonel consents to remain
there as a fixed star, Miss Orpington merely
shrugs her shoulders slightly and expresses no
farther acquiescence.

Life has gone on in all this Arcadian simplicity
for full five weeks, when the appearance of the
Colonel at the breakfast-table, blue frock-coated
and stiff-collared, instead of in the usual easy garb
adopted by him in the country of a morning,
shows some intended change in his proceedings.
The wags of the household, Badger Bobus and
his set, are absent from the breakfast-table; for
there was a heavy billiard-match on the night
before, and they were yet sleeping off its effects.
Nevertheless the change in the Colonel's costume
is not unobserved; but before a delicately-con-
trived question can be put to extract its meaning,
the Colonel himself announces that he has to go
to town for a day, and may possibly be prevented
from returning that night. Modified expressions

of horror from the young ladies and gentlemen about to act in the amateur theatricals, then close impending—fears that everything will go wrong during the manager's absence, and profound distrust of themselves without his suggestions and experience. The Colonel takes these compliments very coolly—is pretty nearly certain to be back that night; and his absence will give them a chance of striking-out any new lights which may occur to them, and which can be tendered for his acceptance on his return. Miss Orpington, when appealed to to persuade her father not to be longer away than is absolutely necessary, meets the matter with her usual shoulder-shrug, and a calm declaration that in those matters she never interferes, and papa always pleases himself.

The Yorkshire baronet with money to whom she is engaged, and who does not put in appearance until after the Colonel's announcement has been made (he was one of those most interested in the billiard-match, and ran Badger Bolus very hard at the last), is really delighted at the news. He and the Colonel get on very well together,

they are on the best of terms both as regards
present and prospective arrangements; but there
is, as Sir George Hawker remarks, something
about the "old boy" which does not "G" with
his, Sir George's, notions of perfect comfort.

Before the last of the dissipated ones has
dropped-in to the dry bacon and leathery toast,
the remnants of the haddocks, and the *débris* of
the breakfast, the Colonel is driving a dog-cart
to the station, where the signal for the express
to stop is already flying. The equanimity which
the old warrior has sustained in the presence of
his friends deserts him a little now when there
is no one near him save a stolid-faced groom
who is gazing vacantly over the adjacent country.
His annoyance does not vent itself on the horse,
he is too good a whip for that; but he "pishes!" and
"pshaws!" and is very short and sharp with the
groom demanding orders as he leaves his master
at the station; and when he has been sucked-up,
as it were, into the train, which is again thun-
dering on its townward way, he takes a letter
from his pocket, and daintily adjusting his natty

double-eyeglass on his nose, reads it through and through.

" This is the infernal nuisance of having to make women allies in matters of this kind," says he softly to himself, laying down the letter and looking out of the window. " They are always doing too much or too little ; anything like a *juste milieu* seems to be utterly impossible to them ; and I cannot make out from this girl's rodomontade nonsense whether she has not just overstepped her instructions, and so spoiled what promised to be a remarkably pretty little plot. And yet it was the only thing I could do, and she was the only available person. It was a thousand pities that Clarisse was away from town at the moment; for she is not merely thoroughly trustworthy, but always has her wits about her."

When the train arrives in London, the Colonel calls a cab, and is driven to the Beaufort Club, which is still empty and deserted, and where he asks the porter whether certain members, whom he names, had been there lately. Among these names is that of Mr. Derinzy; and on being ans-

wered in the negative, he brightens up a little
and pursues his way. This time the cabman is
directed to drive to the Temple; and at the
Temple gates he stops and deposits his fare.

There are symptoms of renewing life among
the lawyers, for term-time is coming on. As the
Colonel steps down Middle Temple-lane, he passes
by long ladders, and has to skip out of the way of
the shower of whitewash and water, which the
painters, standing on them, scatter refreshingly
about. It is for Seldon-buildings that Colonel
Orpington is making; and arrived in that quiet
little nook, where the hum of the many-footed
passing up and down Fleet-street sounds only
like the distant roar of the sea, he stops before
the doorway of No. 5, and after a rapid glance
upwards, to assure himself that he is right, enters the house, and climbs the dingy staircase.
The clerks in the attorney's office on the ground-
floor seem to be in full swing; but the oak on
the first-floor, guarding the chambers where Tocsin, Q.C., gets himself in training for gladiatorial
practice is closed, Tocsin being still away. Arrived

at the second-floor, the Colonel pauses to take breath, the ascent having been a little steep. There are two doors, one on either hand, and both are closed. After a moment's breathing space, the Colonel turns to the one on the right, which bears the name of "Mr. John Wilson;" and after a short glance round, to see that he is unobserved—it was scarcely worth the trouble, for he was most certain there would be none there to see him—he takes a neat little Bramah-key from his pocket, opens the oak, and entering, closes it carefully behind him. There is nothing in the little hall but a stone filter and a couple of empty champagne-bottles. So the Colonel does not linger there, but quickly passing through, opens the door in front of him, and finds himself in a large room dimly lit, by reason of the window-blinds being all pulled down. When these are raised—and to raise them is the Colonel's first proceeding—he looks round him with a shiver, lights a fire, which is already laid in the grate, and carelessly glances round the apartment. Not like a lawyer's rooms these; not like the office of a hard-working attorney, the chambers of a hard-reading, many-brief-getting barrister; not like the chambers of Tocsin, Q.C.—even though Tocsin notoriously goes in for luxury, and affects to be a swell; no litter of many papers here, no big bundles of briefs, no great sheets of parchment, no tin boxes painted with resonant names (in most cases as fictitious as the drawers of Mr. Bob Sawyer's chemist-shop), no legal library bound in calf, no wig-box, no stuff-gown refreshingly dusted with powder hanging up behind the door. Elegant furniture, more like that found in a Mayfair drawing-room than in the purlieus of the Temple: long looking-glasses from floor to ceiling, velvet-covered mantelpiece, china gimcrackery placed here and there, easy-chairs and sofa; no writing-table, but a little davenport of old black oak, a round dining-table capable of seating six persons, a heavy sideboard also in black oak, and a dumb-waiter. Heavy cloth curtains, relieved by an embroidered border, cover the windows; and on the walls are proofs after Landseer. Thick dust is over all; and as the fire is slow in lighting, the Colonel shivers again as

he gives it a vicious poke, and says to himself,

"'Gad! there is a horrible air of banquet-halls
deserted, and all that kind of thing, about the
place! It must be more than three months since
any one was in it. When was the last time, by
the way? O, when I gave Grenville and Browne
and Harriet that supper after the picnic." The
fire struggles up a little, but the Colonel still
shivers. "I wish I had told that old woman who
attends to this place that Mr. Wilson was likely to
be here for an hour or two to-day, and wanted his
fire lit. I hope my young friend will be punctual.
It is better down at Harbledown than at this
dreary place; and it wouldn't do for me to show
in town—not that there is anybody here to see
me, I suppose. Young Derinzy away still—that
is good hearing; but what could she have meant
by 'things not looking very straight'? Always
so confoundedly enigmatical and mysterious in
her writing. Perhaps she will be more explicit
when we meet face to face." Then, looking at his
watch, "Let me see—just two; and I have not

time to get any luncheon anywhere; that is to
say, if she comes at the hour which I telegraphed
to her."

The fire is burning bravely now, and the
Colonel is bending over it, rejoicing in its warmth,
when he hears a slight tinkling of a bell. He
looks up and listens.

" 'Gad! I forgot I had closed the oak," he
says. " I come here so seldom, that the ways of
these places are still strange to me." (Tinkle
again.) " That must be my young friend."

He rises leisurely, crosses the hall, and opens
the door, and is confronted by a tall young woman, rather flashily dressed, who lifts her veil,
and reveals the features of Miss Bella Merton, the
clerk at Mr. Kammerer's, the photographer.

" Is Mr. Wilson in, sir?" asked the young
lady, with a demure glance.

" He is," said the Colonel; " and delighted to
welcome you to his rooms. Come in, my dear
young lady; there is no necessity for either of us
acting a part now. You are very punctual, and
in matters of business — and ours is entirely

a matter of business — that is a very excellent sign."

He led her into the room, pulled an arm-chair opposite the fire, and handed her to it.

"I scarcely know whether I am doing right in coming here, Colonel Orpington," said Bella Merton—"by myself, you know, and alone with a gentleman," she added, as if in reply to his wondering look.

"I mentioned just now that there was no necessity for any nonsense between us, Miss Merton," said the Colonel quietly, "and that we are engaged on what is purely a matter of business. Let us understand each other exactly. You are my agent, my paid agent—I don't wish to hurt your feelings, but in business frankness is everything—to make inquiries and act for me in a certain matter, and you have come here to make me your report. There is no mystery about it so far as you are concerned, except that you are to know me in it as Mr. Wilson ; but you will find, my dear Miss Merton, as you grow older, that in many of the most important business transactions in the world the name of the principal is not allowed to transpire.   Do I make myself clear?"

Miss Merton, though still young, has plenty of *savoir-faire*.   She takes her cue at once; lays aside her giggling, demure and blushing friskiness, and comes to the point.

"Perfectly, Mr. Wilson," she replied.   "I received your telegram, and am here obedient to it."

"That is very right, very prompt, and very much to the purpose," says the Colonel.   "I ask you to meet me here, because in your note received this morning you seem to intimate that things were not going quite as comfortable as I could wish with our young friend—Fanny, I think you call her.   Is not that her name?"

"Yes; Fanny Stafford."

"Very well, then; in future we will always speak of her as Fanny, or Miss Stafford, as occasion may require.   Will you be good enough now to enter into farther particulars?"

"Well, you see, Mr. Wilson"—and the girl cannot help smiling as she repeats his name, for

Colonel Orpington looks so utterly unlike any possible Mr. Wilson—"Fanny has grown dull and out of sorts lately; and I cannot help thinking, from some words she has occasionally dropped, that she is anxious to leave Madame Clarisse, and settle herself in life."

"I don't know that I should prove any obstacle to that," says the Colonel; "it would depend, of course, on the manner in which she proposed to settle herself."

"Of course," says the girl, looking at him keenly; "that is just it; and, if I may be excused for saying so, I don't think hers was in your way."

"Very likely not. Please understand you are to say everything and anything that comes into your head and you think relates to the business we have in hand. I imagine, from the hint in your letter, that the gentleman of whom we have spoken, Mr.—how do you call him?"

"Mr. Douglas—Paul Douglas."

"Ay, Mr. Douglas—had come to town. On inquiry, I find this is not the case."

" No, but she hears from him constantly; and though she never shows me his letters, I can gather from what she says that there has been something in the last one or two of them which has upset her very much."

" You have not the least idea what this something may be?   Do you imagine he proposes to break with her?"

" On the contrary, I think she discovers that his love for her is even deeper than she imagined, and I think that her conscience is reproaching her a little in regard to him."

The Colonel looks up astonished.

" Who can have benefited by any lapse or waywardness of which these conscience-stings can be the result?" he asks.   " Not I, for one."

" I don't think any one is benefited by them, Colonel Orpington," says the girl, with a shadow on her face; " I am sure no one has in the way you suggested.   What I mean is this, that Fanny is naturally discontented with her position, and anxious for riches, and fine clothes, and a pretty home, and all that.   Since I have talked to her

about you and the strong admiration you have for
her, and your coming after her photograph, and
giving Mr. Kammerer the heavy price he asked
for it, and constantly speaking to me about her,
she has grown more discontented still, I fancy;
and we women can generally read each other's
minds and guess at each other's ideas, principally
from the fact that we are all made use of and
played upon in the same way, I imagine.   I fancy
that Fanny thinks that she has not acted quite
fairly towards Paul Douglas since his absence;
that all this talk about you has lessened her regard for him, and led her to picture to herself
another future than that which she contemplated
when he went away, and—   Well, I have rather
an idea that there is another disturbing element
in the matter."

    "'Gad!" says the Colonel, stroking his mous-
tache thoughtfully, "there seems to be quite
enough complication as it is.   What is it now?"

    "I fancy that a young man in her own station
of life, bright, active, and industrious, and likely
to make a very good position for himself in that

station out of which he would never want to move—
for he is proud of it, and thoroughly self-reliant—
is deeply smitten with Fanny, and that she knows
it."

The Colonel looks up relieved.

" I wouldn't give much for this young man's
chance, pattern of all the virtues though he may
be.   I don't think he is much in Miss Stafford's
line."

" Perhaps not," says Bella Merton, " nor do I
think he would be likely to succeed, if Fanny had
not several sides to her character.   At all events,
whether he succeeds or not, the knowledge that
he cares for her, and that he is ready to open a
new career for her, has an irritating and upsetting
effect upon her just now."

The Colonel lit a cigar during the progress of
this dialogue, and sat smoking it thoughtfully.

" Do you happen to know whether Madame
Clarisse is in town?" he asks her after a few
minutes' pause.

" I think I heard Fanny say that she came
back from Paris last week," replies Miss Merton;

"yes, I am sure she did; for I recollect Fanny
telling me Madame had said that she might have
a holiday, and I wanted her to come away with
me to get a change somewhere."

"Quite right of you to throw yourself as much
with her as possible; but don't take her away just
yet. You have given me most admirable aid, Miss
Merton, and have managed this affair with a delicacy and discretion which do you infinite credit,
and which I shall never forget. Will you add to
your favour?"

"Willingly, if I can, Colonel—I mean Mr.
Wilson," says Bella, with a blush. "How is it
to be done?"

"By getting yourself a dress, or mantle, or
something of that new brown colour which is just
come into fashion, about which all the ladies are
raving, and which I am sure would become you
admirably, and by wearing it the next time I have
the pleasure of receiving a visit from you," says
the Colonel, pressing a bank-note into his visitor's hand. "And now good-bye. Not a word of
thanks; I told you at the beginning this was a

mere matter of business; I am merely carrying out my words."

"You wish me still to see Fanny, and to let you know anything that may transpire?" asks Bella.

"Certainly; though perhaps I may soon— However, never mind; write always to the same address, and keep me well informed."

Miss Merton goes tripping through the Temple, in great delight at the crisp little contents of her purse that she has just received from the Colonel, and commanding great tribute of admiration from the attorneys' clerks who catch glimpses of her through the grimy windows behind which they are working; and Colonel Orpington, *alias* Mr. John Wilson, sits with his feet before him on the fender, smoking slowly, and cogitating over all he has heard.

It is dusk in the Temple precincts, though still bright light outside, before he rises from his chair, flings the butt-end of his last cigar into the fire, and says to himself,

"Yes, I think that I must now appear on

the scene myself, and see how the land lies with my own eyes. I wonder whether young Derinzy has been playing this recent game from forethought or by accident. Deuced clever move of his if he intended it; but I rather think it was all a chance; such knowledge of life does not come to one until after a great deal of experience, and he is a mere boy as yet. I don't think much of what my young friend just now said about the tradesman, artisan, or whatever the fellow may happen to be, though she seemed to have a notion that he would prove dangerous. However, it will all work out in time, I suppose. I won't stop in town to-night, now there is nothing to be done; the house in Hill-street is all upset, and I will go back to my comfortable quarters at Harbledown, and give those acting people the benefit of my society. John Orpington," he says, looking at himself in the glass over the mantelpiece, "you have come to a time of life when rest is absolutely necessary for you, and you have got too much good sense to ignore the fact; and as to Miss Fanny Stafford, well,—*la nuit porte conseil,*—I will sleep upon all I have heard, and make up my mind to-morrow morning." And so little excited or flurried is Colonel Orpington by the events of the day, that when the down express is stopped by signal at the little station, the guard, previously charged to look out for him, finds the Colonel deep in slumber over his evening newspaper.

CHAPTER VII.

WELL MET.

In her light and volatile way, Miss Bella Merton
had made what was by no means a wrong estimate
of Daisy's state of mind; more especially right
was she in her conjecture that Paul Derinzy's absence had had the effect of showing to Daisy the
true state of her feelings towards him, and that
she found her heart much more complicated than
she had believed. She had been accustomed to
those walks in Kensington-gardens, which had
become of almost daily occurrence, and she missed
them dreadfully. She had been accustomed to
the soft words, the tender speeches, to the little
pettings and fondlings and delicate attentions
which her lover was always paying to her, and in
her solitude she hungered after them. True, his
letters were all that a girl in her position could

desire—full of the kindest phrases and most affectionate reminiscences, full of delight at the past and of hope for the future; only, after all, they were but letters, and Daisy wearied of his absence and longed for his return.

In the dull dead season of the year, when everything was weary and melancholy, when business was at such a stand-still that she had not even the excitement of her work to carry off her thoughts in another direction, the girl pondered over her lot, and the end of each period of reflection found her heartily sick of it. How long was it to endure? Was this daily slavery to go on for ever? Was she still to live in a garret, to emerge from thence in the early morning to the dull routine of business, to go through the daily toil of showing her employer's wares to listless customers, of enduring all their vapid impertinences and senseless remarks, to superintend making up the boxes and the sending-off of the parcels, and to return again to the cheerless garret, weary, dispirited, and dead-beat? So that slight glimpse of the promised land which had been accorded to her when she first made up her mind that she would bring Paul's attentions to a definite end, that marriage never to be perfectly realised while he was with her, while she was in the daily habit of meeting him and listening to his impassioned words, that future which she had depicted to herself, seemed now perfectly possible of realisation, although Paul had, as she was compelled to allow to herself, never held out definite hopes of marrying her, but contented himself by dwelling on the impossibility of any decadence in his love, or of his being able to pass his life away from her.

But since his absence in the country these pleasant visions had gradually faded and grown colourless. Thinking over the past, Daisy was compelled to allow to herself that, though their acquaintance now extended over some months, the great end to which she was looking forward seemed as far off as ever. Who were those people of his, as he called them? this family of whom he apparently stood in such awe? and even if their consent were obtained, would Paul have courage enough

to fly in the face of the world by marrying a girl
in a station of life inferior to his own? The moral
cowardice on this point she was aware of; his
weakness she knew. She had seen it in his avoid-
ance of public places when in her company, and
the constant fright of detection which he laboured
under. She had taxed him with it, and he could
not deny it, but laughed it off as best he might.
He even in laughing it off had confessed that he
stood in wholesome terror of Mrs. Grundy and all
the remarks which she and her compeers might
make. Was this a feeling likely to be effaced by
time? She thought not. The older he grew the
less likely was he to care to defy the world's opinion, unsustained as he would be by the first
fierce strength of that love which alone could spur
him on to what was, in his eyes, a deed of such
daring.

And Daisy was in this position, that, however
much she might seem to talk and laugh with
Bella Merton. she could not take that young person, nor indeed any person of her own age, into
her confidence. All the counsel and advice which

she had to rely on must come from her mother alone, and Mrs. Stothard's advice was like herself, grim and very hard and very worldly. From the first she had seemed much pleased with Daisy's account of her relations with Paul. She had urged her daughter to persevere in the course on which she had decided, and to lose no opportunity for making the young man declare himself, so that they might have some legal hold upon him. All this was to be done cautiously and without hurry, so long as he continued as attached as he then seemed to be. Daisy was cautioned against doing anything which might alarm him; it was only if she perceived that he was relaxing in his attentions that she was at once to endeavour to bring him to book.

And though Daisy was fully aware that her more recent letters to her mother, written since Paul's absence, had been influenced by the dulness which that event had caused her, and were, in truth, nothing but reassuring productions, Mrs. Stothard's had never lost heart. They were cheerful and hopeful; bade her daughter not to give way, as she felt certain that all would be right in the end; and were full of a spirit of gaiety which was little characteristic of the writer.

And there were two other influences at work which tended to disturb Daisy's peace of mind. Her acquaintance Bella Merton, though sufficiently social and volatile, had a singular knack of persistence in carrying through any plan on which she might be engaged; and since the subject was first mentioned at the little party in Augusta Manby's rooms, she had taken advantage of every opportunity of being in Daisy's company, to enlarge to her on Colonel Orpington's position and generosity, and of the extraordinary admiration which he had professed for Fanny's portrait and herself.

These remarks were listened to by Daisy at first with unconcern, and their perpetual iteration would probably have disgusted her, had not Miss Merton been endowed with an unusual amount of feminine tact, and thus enabled to serve them up in a manner which she thought would be peculiarly palatable to her friend; so that Daisy found

herself not merely constantly listening to stories
of Colonel Orpington when she was in Miss Merton's company, but thinking a great deal of that
distinguished individual when she was alone. She
had taken very little notice of him on the day
when he called in George-street with his daughter,
and could only recollect of his personal appearance that it was gentlemanly and distinguished
looking; but she remembered having noticed the
keen way in which he looked at her, and one
glance of unmistakable admiration which he
levelled at her as he followed his daughter from
the room. And he was very rich, was he? and
very generous—very generous? Why was Bella
Merton always harping on his generosity? why
was she always talking in a vague way of hoping
some day to be able to introduce him formally?

To Daisy there could be no misunderstanding
about the purpose of such an introduction, the
girl thought, with flaming cheek; and the recollection of Paul's delicacy came across her, and she
felt enraged with herself at ever having permitted
Bella Merton to talk to her in that fashion. And

yet—and yet what was the remainder of her life to be, Paul making no sign? She knew perfectly well that that little tea-party in Dalston-road might, in another way, take rank as an epoch in her life. She knew perfectly well that John Merton, who had always admired her, that night had yielded up his heart, and she would not have been surprised any day at receiving an offer of his hand. Was that to be the end of it? Was she to pull down the image of Paul, which she worshipped so fondly, and erect that of homely John Merton in its place? Was she to continue in very much the same style of life which she was then leading, merely exchanging her garret for a room a little less high, a little better furnished, but probably in a less desirable part of the town? Was she to remain as a drudge—not indeed to Madame Clarisse or any other employer, for she knew John Merton was too high spirited to think of allowing her to help towards their mutual maintenance by her own labour—but still as a drudge in domestic duties, in slavery for children and household, never to rise in the social scale, never to know anything of those luxuries which she so longed for? It was a bitter, bitter trial, and the more Daisy thought it over— and the question was constantly present in her mind—the less chance did she see of bringing it to a satisfactory conclusion.

Although the professional people whose duties required their attendance in town were beginning to come back, and bringing with them, of course, their wives and families, the majority of Madame Clarisse's more happily placed customers yet remained in their country houses, and there was still very little business doing at the establishment in George-street. There were frequently times in the day when Daisy had nothing to do, and she would take advantage of her leisure to go out and get a breath of the bleak autumnal air. Madame Clarisse never objected to these little excursions; indeed, encouraged them. For on her return from France, she had noticed that her favourite Fanfan's cheeks were looking very pale, and that her manner was listless and dispirited, and that she plainly wanted a change. Madame was at first disposed to insist on Fanfan's going

away for a time to the country or the seaside, and
recruiting herself amid fresh scenes.   But a communication which she received about that period
altered her views ; and she consequently contented
herself by giving her assistant as many hours'
leisure as she conveniently could, taking care that
this leisure was fragmentary, and never to be enjoyed for longer than one afternoon at a time.

Daisy had an odd delight, when thus enabled
to absent herself from her duties, in visiting the
old spot in Kensington-gardens which had been
the scene of her walks with Paul.   They had
selected it on account of its seclusion, but now
there were fewer people there than ever ; it was
too damp and cold any longer to be used as a
place of recreation by the children who formerly
frequented it for its quietude and its shade; and
an occasional workman hurrying across the Park,
or a keeper, finding his occupation gone in the
absence of the boys, gazing wearily down the
long vistas at the end of which the thick white
fog was already beginning to steam, were the
only human creatures whom Daisy encountered.

She was astonished, therefore, one day, on arriving at the end of the well-known avenue, and turning to retrace her steps, to find herself face to face with a gentleman who must evidently have made his approach under cover of the trees, and who was close to her before she had heard his footfall.

She recognised him in an instant—Colonel Orpington.

"I must ask your pardon for intruding on you, Miss Stafford," said the Colonel, raising his hat, "and more especially for having come upon you so suddenly, and caused, as I am afraid I see by your startled looks, some annoyance; but though I have never had the pleasure of a personal introduction, we have met before, and I believe you know who I am."

His manner was perfectly easy and gentlemanly, but thoroughly respectful withal; and though, as he had noticed, Daisy's first impulse was to turn aside and leave him without a word, a moment's reflection caused her to bow and say,

"I believe I recognise Colonel Orpington."

"Exactly; and in Colonel Orpington you see an unfortunate man who is compelled, from what the begging-letter writers call in their flowery language 'circumstances over which he has no control,' to remain in London at this horribly dismal time of year."

Daisy was silent, but she smiled; and the Colonel proceeded:

"I wandered into the Park and strolled up the Row, where there were only three men, who were apparently endeavouring to see which could hold on to their horses longest; and I was comparing the ghastliness of to-day with the glory of last season—I need not quote to you, I am sure, my dear Miss Stafford, that charming notion about a 'sorrow's crown of sorrows,' which Mr. Tennyson so cleverly copied from Mr. Dante, who thought of it first—when at the far end by the Serpentine-bridge I got a glimpse of a form which I thought I recognised, and which, if I may say so, has never been absent from my mind since I first saw it. I made bold to follow it;

and just now, on your turning round, I found I was right in my conjectures. It was you."

He paused; but Daisy did not smile now, merely bowed stiffly, and moved as though she would proceed. The Colonel moved at the same time.

" I hope you are not annoyed at my freedom, Miss Stafford," said he. " Believe me, at the smallest hint from you, I will rid you of my presence this instant; but it does seem rather ridiculous that two persons, who, I think we are not flattering in saying, are calculated to amuse one another at a time and in a place where they are as much alone as the grand old gardener and his wife were in Paradise, should avoid each other in an eminently British manner, simply because conventionality does not recognise their meeting."

This time Daisy smiled, almost laughed, as she said, " You will readily understand, Colonel Orpington, that the rules of society have no great hold upon me, who have never been in any position to be bound by them; and I haven't the least objection to your walking part of the way with me on my return to my employer's, if it at all pleases or amuses you to do so."

"It would give me the very greatest pleasure," said the Colonel; and they walked on together.

As Daisy looked up for an instant at the face of her companion and thought of Paul, she could not help wondering at the contrast between the two men: he with whom she had been in the habit of walking up and down that avenue was always so thoroughly in earnest, his head bent down in fond solicitude towards her, his eyes seeking hers, every tone of his voice, every movement of his hands showing how deeply interested he was in that one subject on which alone they talked; while her present companion, though probably fully double Paul's age, walked along gaily and blithely, his head erect, and his voice and manner as his conversation.

"This is really charming," said the Colonel. "I had not the least idea of so pleasant an interview in my dull dreary day; there is literally not one soul in London of my acquaintance, except yourself, Miss Stafford; and do you know, on reflection, I am rather glad of it."

"Indeed; and why, Colonel Orpington?"

"Because, don't you know, they say that people who in the whirl of the season might be constantly coming into momentary contact, and then carried away off somewhere else, never have the slightest opportunity of really becoming acquainted with each other; whereas, when people are thrown together at this time of year and this kind of way, there is a chance for their discovering each other's best qualities, and thus establishing an intimacy."

· Daisy laughed again; this time a rather hard bitter laugh.

"You forget, Colonel Orpington, you are talking to me now as though I am one whom you are likely to meet in the whirl of the season, one with whom you are likely to become on intimate terms."

The Colonel looked grave. "I am thinking that you have the manners, the appearance, and the education of a lady, Miss Stafford; you could have nothing more," said he quietly. "And now, where are you bound for?"

"I am going back to my employer's in George-street."

"Ah, Madame Clarisse's, where I had first the pleasure of seeing you. And does that still go on, Miss Stafford, every day—that same work in which I saw you engaged?"

"Exactly the same, day after day," said Daisy with a little sigh; "a little less of it now, a little more of it another time, but always the same."

"'Gad, it must be dull," said the Colonel, pulling down the corners of his mouth, "having to show a lot of gowns and things to pert young misses and horrible old women, and listen to their wretched jargon. Don't you sometimes feel inclined to tell them plainly what frights they are, and how the fault, when they find fault, is not in the thing—cap, ribbon, shawl, or whatever it may be—which they are trying on, but in themselves?"

"Madame Clarisse would scarcely thank me for that, I think," said Daisy; "and I should rather repent my own folly when I found myself

without employment, and without recommendation necessary for getting it."

"Yes, of course, you are right," said the
Colonel, "it would not do; but the temptation
must be awfully strong. I was thinking after I
left Clarisse's the other day, how astonished the
hideous creatures who go there must be when
they find that the things which look so charming
on you when you were showing them off, so entirely lost their charm when sent home to the
persons who have purchased them. Like a fairy
tale, by Jove!" As he said this, Colonel Orpington
cast a momentary glance at his companion to see
what effect his remarks had produced, and was
pleased to find that Daisy looked gratified. The
next moment her countenance clouded as she
said,

"It is not a very ennobling position, that of
being an animated block for showing the effect
of milliner's wares, but I suppose there are worse
in the world."

"Of course there are, my dear Miss Stafford:
many worse, and a great many better. It would

be a dreary look-out, though, if you had no brighter future in store for you."

" It is a dreary look-out, then," said the girl, almost solemnly.

" Don't say that," said the Colonel, moving a little closer towards her, and slightly lowering his voice; " you mustn't talk in that manner; you are depressed by the dull time, and the day, and this charming fog which is now rising steadily around us. You don't imagine, I suppose, that the rest of your life is to be spent at Madame Clarisse's ?"

" At Madame Clarisse's, or Madame Augustine's, or Madame somebody else's, I suppose," said Daisy.

" But have you no idea of setting-up in business for yourself?" asked the Colonel. " It would not be any great position, but at all events it would be better than this. At any time, I imagine, it is more pleasant to drive than to be driven."

" I have never thought of it," said the girl; " the chance is so very remote, it does not do to look forward. I find it is better to go on simply from day to day, taking it all as it comes," said Daisy with a short laugh.

"Now, my dear Miss Stafford, you really must not speak in that way. I must take advantage of my being, unfortunately, a great deal older than you, and having seen a great deal more of the world, to give you a little advice, and to talk seriously to you. You are far too young, and, permit me to add, far too beautiful, to hold such gloomy and desponding views. From the little I have already had the pleasure of seeing of you, I should say you were eminently calculated by the charm—well, the charm of your appearance—for there is no denying that with us ordinary denizens of the world, who are not philosophers, a charming appearance goes a long way—and of your manners, you are eminently calculated to make friends who would only be delighted at an opportunity of serving you."

"Such has not been my experience at present," said the girl. "I am afraid that your desire to be polite has led you into error, Colonel Orpington; I find no such friends as you describe."

"I was mistaken," said the Colonel; "I thought there must be at least one person who would have done anything for you."

As he said these words, he looked sharply at her; and though Daisy's eyes were downcast, she noticed the glance, and felt that she blushed under it.

"However, be that as it may," said the Colonel, "it will be my care to see that you are unable to make that assertion henceforth. Believe me, that this day you have made a friend whose greatest delight will be in forwarding your every wish."

He dropped his voice as he said these words, and let his hand for an instant rest lightly on hers.

"You are very kind," she said, "and I know I ought to be very grateful—I ought."

"You ought not to say another word, Miss Stafford," said the Colonel. "When you are a little older and a little more experienced, you will know that there is nothing more foolish than to be too ready with your gratitude. Wait and see what comes. Think over what I have said, and settle in your own mind in what way I can be of service to you; and don't be angry with me for saying that you must not be afraid to take me literally at my word. Fortune, who is so hard upon many excellent and deserving people, has been especially kind to me, who don't deserve anything at all, and I have much more money than I can spend upon myself. Think over all I have said, and let me look forward to the pleasure of seeing you in the same spot again to-morrow afternoon. Now I will intrude upon you no longer. Good-bye."

He touched her hand, took off his hat, and before Daisy could speak a word, he had left her, and was retracing his steps across the Park.

CHAPTER VIII.

CAPTAIN DERINZY did not experience so much satisfaction as he had anticipated from Mr. George Wainwright's visit to the Tower. On the first night of his arrival, his guest had listened to him with the greatest patience and apparent delight. The Captain had told all his old stories, repeated his *bon mots*—which were very brilliant some dozen years before, but had lost a little of their glitter and piquancy—and had aired the two subjects on which he was strongest—his delight in London life, and his disgust at the place in which he was then compelled to vegetate—to his own entire satisfaction.

He had hoped for frequent renewals of these pleasant confabulations during George Wainwright's stay; but the next morning Paul told his father that he and his friend had matters of business to talk over; and although George seemed willing, and even anxious, to give up portions of his time occasionally to his host, he was so much in requisition by Paul, by Annette, and even by Mrs. Stothard, that the poor Captain found himself left as much as usual to his own devices, and wandered about the beach and the cliffs, cursing his fate and his exile as loudly as ever. But while he was thus excluded from the general councils, a series of explanations seemed to be going on among the other members of the household.

"I want to speak to you, Martha," said Mrs. Derinzy, on the afternoon of the day after the conversation last recorded had taken place. "I have been thinking over what you said this morning, and I want you to be more explicit about it."

"About what portion of it?" asked Mrs. Stothard.

"Well, about all; but more particularly what you said about my only having chosen to give you half confidences. What did you mean by that?"

"Exactly what I said. You're a clever woman, Mrs. Derinzy, but you have made a great mistake in imagining that you could make me a fellow-conspirator with you in a plot—"

"Conspirator! plot!" cried Mrs. Derinzy, interrupting.

"Exactly. A fellow-conspirator in a plot," said Mrs. Stothard calmly—"I use the words advisedly—and yet only tell me a portion of your intentions."

"Will you be good enough to explain yourself, Mrs. Stothard?" said Mrs. Derinzy, seating herself, and thereby asserting her superiority in the only way possible over her servant, who knew so much, and was apparently inclined to make a dangerous use of her knowledge.

"Certainly," said Mrs. Stothard. "I am the only person in this place, besides you and your husband, who knows that your niece Annette Derinzy is subject to fits of lunacy. I say who *knows* it; it may be suspected more or less, though I don't think it is much. But I know it. The fact is kept sedulously by you from all who are

likely to be brought in contact save the one physician who attends, and his visits are accounted
for by a pretext that you, and not Annette, are his
patient. If that is not a plot in which we are
fellow-conspirators, I should like to know what
is."

"Go on," said Mrs. Derinzy in a low voice.

"I am going on," said Mrs. Stothard pitilessly.
"The reason for your concealing the fact that this
girl is an occasional lunatic is, that she is the
heiress of a very large fortune, and that since the
day on which you first heard of her inheritance
you determined that she should marry your only
son. For my discovery of this portion of the plot,
I am not indebted to you. It was the work entirely of my own observation. You can say
whether I am right in my conjecture or not."

"Suppose you are, what then?"

"Suppose I am! What is the use of beating
about the bush in this absurd way any longer?
You know I am right. Now that you see the
difficulty of blinding your son any longer to his
cousin's condition, and that he is not weak enough

to have been played upon to any extent, had it not
been for the influence which this newly-arrived
friend has over him, you find that you require my
aid, and want my advice."

Perhaps for the first time in her long scheming anxious life Mrs. Derinzy felt herself thoroughly prostrate. She hid her face in her hands,
and when she raised it, tears were streaming down
her cheeks.   She made no farther attempt at concealment of her feelings, but murmured piteously,
" What are we to do, Martha—what are we to
do?"

Mrs. Stothard's hard face softened for a moment as she stepped towards her, and touched her
gently with her hand.

" What are you to do!" she cried.   " Not to
give way like this, and throw up all chance of
winning the battle after so long and desperate a
fight.   Let us think it over quietly, see exactly
how matters stand, and determine what can be
done for the best."

" He must never know it, Martha—he must
never know it !" murmured Mrs. Derinzy.

"Who must never know what?" asked Mrs. Stothard shortly.

"Paul must never know that Annette is mad. If he finds it out, of course all hope of his marrying her is at an end. And what will he think of me for having deceived him? — of me, his mother, who did it all for his good."

"You must be rational, or it will be impossible to decide upon anything," said Mrs. Stothard, who had relapsed into her grim state. "As to Paul's not knowing, that is sheer nonsense. I told you long ago, it was very unadvisable to have him down here at all. But he is not very observant, and with proper care might have been easily gulled. The girl was getting better, too—that is to say, there was a longer interval between her attacks, and the matter might possibly have been arranged. Now that Mr. George Wainwright has seen her, and is an inmate of the same house with her, that hope is entirely at an end."

"You think so, Martha?"

"I am certain of it."

"Then all my self-sacrifice, all my anxieties

and schemings have been thrown away, and I have no farther care for life," said Mrs. Derinzy, again bursting into tears.

"You are relapsing into silliness again. Suppose Paul were told of his cousin's illness, do you think he would definitely refuse to marry her ?"

"Instantly and for ever," said Mrs. Derinzy.

"What! if the fact were notified by George Wainwright, who at the same time hinted that though Annette had been insane, her disease was much decreased in violence and frequency during the last few years, and in the next few might possibly cease altogether? Would Paul, hearing all this, and urged on by you, give up his notion of the fortune he would enjoy with his wife—Paul, who is, as I have heard say, so fond of pleasure and enjoyment, so imbued with a passion for spending money ?"

She paused, and Mrs. Derinzy looked at her in astonishment, then said,

"Paul is weak and frivolous, but is no fool ; he will not believe it."

"Not if it is told him by his friend who has such influence over him, and on whose integrity he relies so thoroughly; not if it is told him by Dr. Wainwright's son."

"He might if it were told him by Dr. Wainwright himself," said Mrs. Derinzy, hesitating.

"And don't you think that George Wainwright has sufficient influence with his father to make him do as he wishes?" asked Mrs. Stothard.

"Has any one sufficient influence with George Wainwright to make him help in our scheme?"

"Time will show," said Mrs. Stothard. "Now that we understand each other, I think you had better leave this affair wholly in my hands. You know me well enough to be certain that I shall do my best to serve you."

"That was the best way to settle it," said Mrs. Stothard to herself as she walked towards her own room. "It was necessary to face it out,—it would have been impossible to make her believe that Paul could have been kept in ignorance of the secret. And yet she is weak enough to think a man like George Wainwright

would suffer himself to take part in such a
wretched scheme as this, and compromise his
own honour and his friend's happiness! However,
it will amuse her, and give me time to mature my
own plans. I rather think the notion that I hit
on this morning will be the best one to work out
after all; the best one, that is to say, for all I care
—for Fanny and myself. Ah, who is this coming
in from the garden? It is Mr. Wainwright. I
wonder what he thinks of me; his look last night
was anything but flattering; now we shall see.
—Good-morning, sir."

"Good-morning to you, nurse; how is your
charge this morning?"

"My charge? O, you mean Miss Annette.
She's very well indeed; I think she seems to
have benefited very much by the change which
the arrival of company has brought to the house."

"Company! Mr. Paul can scarcely be considered company in his own home, and I fear I
am not much company."

"It doesn't sound very flattering, Mr. Wainwright; but the mere sight of a fresh face does

us good in this dull place. I always tell Mrs. Derinzy that my young lady wants rousing; and I am sure I am right, for it is a long time since I have seen her look so bright as she does this morning."

"I am sure you are not sufficiently selfish as to keep all her brightness to yourself, nurse," said George; "but I do not think Miss Derinzy has yet left her room."

"I am going to her now," said Mrs. Stothard, "to persuade her to take a turn in the grounds before luncheon; if I may say you will accompany her, Mr. Wainwright, I am sure she will come at once."

"You may say that I will do so with the very greatest pleasure," said George; and then, after Mrs. Stothard had left him, "A clever woman that, and, if my ideas are correct, just the sort of person for that place. What a wonderful position for them all down here, and how extraordinarily well the secret has been preserved! The girl has a singular charm about her, and yet Paul will be delighted at getting—as I have very little doubt

he will get—his release. Fancy wishing to be
released from— What can have made that woman
so civil to me this morning? I thought I came
down here for quiet, and I find that I must not
move or speak without previously exercising the
most tremendous caution. Ah, here is Miss Annette; how pretty and fresh she looks!"

She did look wonderfully pretty in her tight-
fitting violet-cashmere dress, made high round her
throat, with a small neat white collar and cuffs,
and with a violet ribbon in her hair. Her eyes
were bright and her manner was frank and free as
she walked straight up to George Wainwright, and
holding out her hand, gave him good-morning.

" Good-morning, Miss Derinzy," said George ;
"you are late in coming among us. I was just
asking your servant what had become of you."

"My servant! O, you mean Mrs. Stothard.
Have you been talking to that horrid woman?
What has she been saying to you?"

"You mustn't call her a horrid woman ; she
has been speaking very nicely of you, and said she
would send you to take a turn in the grounds

with me; so I don't think her a horrid woman, of course."

"She is a horrid woman, all the same," said Annette, "and I hate her; though I shall like taking a turn in the grounds with you. Let us come out at once. What a lovely morning!"

"Yes," said George, as they stood on the steps, "but not lovely enough for you to come out without a hat; the air is anything but warm."

"It strikes cold to you Londoners," said Annette, laughing; and as she laughed, her eyes sparkled and her colour came, and George could not help thinking how remarkably pretty she looked; "but I do not feel it one bit too fresh; I hate having anything on my head."

"Do you never wear a hat?"

"Only when I go into the village with Mrs. Derinzy, never here in the grounds. I hate anything that weighs on my head or gives me any sense of oppression there; always when I feel my head hot I think I am going to be ill."

"Ay, I was sorry to hear that you were so frequently an invalid," said George.

"Yes," said the girl, "I often think the house, instead of the Tower, should be called the Hospital. Mrs. Derinzy, you know, is very often ill; so ill sometimes, that Dr. Wainwright has to come from London to see her."

"So I have heard," said George. "Do you know my father?"

"I have seen him very often when he has been down here to visit my aunt."

"He has never attended you, I suppose, Miss Derinzy?" asked George, looking at her closely.

"Dr. Wainwright attended me! O, dear no," said Annette; "there was never any occasion for his doing so."

"Like most unselfish people, you make light of your own troubles," said George, "and exaggerate those of other people."

"No, indeed," said Annette; "my ailments are trifles compared with those of Mrs. Derinzy."

"How do you feel when you are ill?" asked George.

"What a curious man you are! what curious

questions you ask ! Why do you take any interest in me and my ailments ?"

"In you, because—well, I can only say that I find you very interesting," said George, with a smile ; " and in your illness because I am a doctor's son, you know, and understand something of a doctor's work."

"Well, I can scarcely call mine illnesses," said the girl; " for such as they are, I and Mrs. Stothard—the woman you were just talking to—manage them between us. I feel a sort of heavy burning sensation in my brain, a buzzing in my ears, and a dimness of sight; and then I faint away, and I know of nothing that happens, how the time goes by, or what is said or done around me, until I come to myself, and feel, O, so horribly weak and tired !"

" I told you you spoke too lightly of your own ailments, Miss Derinzy," said George, with an earnest, passionate look ; " and this account of what you suffer seems to give me the idea that you require more skilled treatment than can be afforded by Mrs. Stothard, kind though she may be."

"I didn't say she was kind," said the girl sullenly; "I hate her!"

"Has my father never prescribed for you in one of these attacks?"

"Never; and never shall!"

"I hope you don't hate him too?" asked George, with a smile.

"I—I don't like him."

"May I ask why not?"

"I—I can't tell; but his prescribing for me would be of no use, he could do me no good."

"How can you tell that?"

"Because he has happened to come down here by chance to see my aunt when I have been ill, and of course if he could have cured me, they would have asked him to do so."

"Of course," said George. He looked at her steadily, but could glean nothing from the expression on her face, and he changed the subject. "You haven't seen Paul this morning?"

"No, I see very little of him. Before he came down, my aunt talked so much to me about his visit, and said he was so amusing and so delightful, and that I should be so much pleased with him."

" Well ?"

" Now you are asking me questions again. I intended to make you tell me all about London and what the people do there; and we have been out here for half an hour, and talked about nothing but myself. What did you mean by ' well' ?" she added, laughing.

George laughed too.

" I meant, and you found all Mrs. Derinzy's anticipations realised ?"

" Not the least in the world. I don't find my cousin amusing, and I am sure he doesn't talk much; he walks about smoking a pipe and smoothing his moustache with his fingers; and whenever one speaks to him, his thoughts seem to be a long way off, and he has to call them back before he answers you. I told my aunt he was like those people you read of in books, who are in love."

" What did she say to that ?"

" She smiled, and said she had noticed the

same since Paul had been down here, and that very likely that might be the reason."

"You must not be hard on Paul," said George Wainwright, at the same time frowning slightly; "if you knew him as well as I do, you would think him the best fellow in the world."

"I find that that is what is always said of people whom I don't care about," said Annette quietly.

"My father, for instance," said George, with a laugh, "and Mrs. Stothard."

"Of Dr. Wainwright, certainly," said Annette. "My aunt and uncle are never tired of proclaiming his praises; and my aunt has reasons, for I believe it is to his skill that my aunt owes her life; but I never heard any one say anything good of Mrs. Stothard."

"Poor Mrs. Stothard," said George, "she will most likely— Ah, here is the Captain."

The gentleman strolling up the little white path which led over the cliff to the sea was indeed Captain Derinzy, limping along and slashing at the bushes with his cane in his usual military

manner. He looked very much astonished at seeing Annette walking with his guest, and did not
disguise his surprise.

"Hallo!" he said, "you out here! Seldom
you come out into the open air, isn't it?—Be much
better for her if she came out oftener, wouldn't
it, Wainwright? This is the stuff that they talk
about in this country life. Why, in London a
girl goes out and rides in the Row twice a-day, and
walks and rides in Bond-street, and all that kind
of thing, and gets plenty of exercise, don't you
know? Whereas in the country it is so infernally
dirty, and the roads are all so shamefully bad, and
there are such a set of roughs about—tramps and
that kind of people—that girls don't like going
out; and yet they tell you that the country is
more healthy than London! All dam' stuff!"

"Well, Miss Derinzy's looks certainly do credit
to the country, though I regret to hear that they
are not thoroughly to be relied on. She has been
telling me she suffers a great deal from illness."

"O, has she?" said the Captain, looking up
nervously; "the deuce she has!—Look here,

Netty, don't you think you had better go in and dress yourself for dinner, and that kind of thing ? It is quite cold now, and you haven't got any hat, and your aunt might make a row—I mean, mightn't like it, you know.   Run in, there's a good girl; we shall all be in soon.—Don't you go, Wainwright; I want to show you a view from the top of that hill, the Beacon Hill, they call it; it's about the only thing worth seeing in the whole infernal place."

When Captain Derinzy went in to dress for dinner, he said to his wife,

"It is a deuced good thing that I am a long-headed fellow and have my wits about me, and all that kind of thing.   I found this young Wainwright walking with Annette, and he told me she had been telling him about her illness and all that.   So I thought it best to separate 'em at once ; and I sent her off into the house, and took him away to the Beacon Hill, though he seemed to me to be wanting to go after her all the time."

CHAPTER IX.

TWO IN PURSUIT.

THE festivities of Harbledown Hall were at an end, the amateur theatricals had been given—to the great delight of those performing in them, and to the excessive misery of those witnessing them— on two successive nights : the first to the invited neighbouring gentry, the second to the tenantry and servants.   The guests were dispersed to various other country houses, and among them Miss Orp- ington and her father had taken their departure : but not to the same destination ; the young lady, under the chaperonage of her aunt, was going to stay with some people, the head of whose family was an eminent tea-broker in the City, who, some years before, would not have been received into what is called society, but who was now so enor-

mously rich that society found it could not possibly do without him. Society dined with him
and danced with him at his house in Hyde-park-
gardens, invited his wife and his daughter to all
sorts of entertainments during the season, voted
his two ugly dumpy sons the pleasantest fellows
in Europe, and went regularly to stay with him
during the autumn at his most charming country
place at Brookside near Hastings.

As an acknowledgment of all these kindnesses
the tea-broker had caused himself to be put into
Parliament, and took his place with tolerable
punctuality amongst the conscript fathers, never
failed in obedience to the suggestions of the whip
of his party, and, when he was not in the smoking-
room, sleeping the sleep of the righteous on the
back benches of the House.

The party at Brookside promised this year to
be a particularly agreeable one; and as Miss Orpington had arranged for an introduction with the
Yorkshire baronet with money, and that gentleman
saw his way to unlimited sport during the day
and unlimited flirtation during the evening, they

agreed to console themselves even for the absence of the young lady's papa.

For Colonel Orpington was not going to Brookside. His daughter, as he said, had her aunt to look after her, and her intended to amuse her; and though there was nothing to be said against Skegby—that being the name of the tea-broker—who was a very good fellow, a self-made man, honour to British commerce, and that kind of thing, and was received everywhere, yet there were some people going to Brookside that the Colonel didn't care about meeting; and so, as the house in Hill-street was ready, he should go and take up his quarters there for a time, at all events until he had occasion to inspect the works and quarries in South Wales.

All his friends being still away from London, it was natural that the Colonel should seek for consolation in the resources of that new acquaintance which he had so recently made. He had met Fanny Stafford several times in the Park, and she had so far relaxed from her rigid formality as to accept two or three little dinners from him,

as good as his taste could command and Verrey
could supply, at which Madame Clarisse was always present.

That worthy lady's interest in her assistant
seemed to have increased very much since her
return from Paris. She was always insisting on
Fanny's taking half-holidays, giving up work now
and again, and coming into her private rooms for
a meal and a chat; and in that chat, which was
entirely one-sided and carried on solely by Madame Clarisse, the theme was always the same—
the misery of work and poverty, the glory of idleness and riches, the folly, the worse than folly,
almost crime, of those who spend their life in toil,
and neglect to clutch the golden opportunity which
comes to most all of us when we are young, and
comes but once.

With these remarks—which might have seemed
sententious in any one else, but which Madame
Clarisse put so aptly and so deftly, with such
quaint illustrations, sounding quainter still in the
broken English with which she interlarded her
discourse, as to render it amusing—was often mixed

a series of running comments on Colonel Orpington, which were laudatory, but in which the praise
was laid on with a very skilful hand.

It is due to the Colonel to say that he left
all mention of himself, whether laudatory or
otherwise, to Madame Clarisse, and this was one
of the greatest reasons for which Daisy liked
him.

Beyond referring occasionally to his originally
expressed desire to see the girl removed into some
better position than that which she then occupied,
and his readiness to help her in the achievement
of such a position, Colonel Orpington never seemed
to have any object in his never-failing pursuit of
the girl's acquaintance beyond the perfectly legi-
timate one of amusing himself and her, and making
the time pass pleasantly for them both. He was
always gay, always cheerful, always full of good-
humoured talk and anecdote, but at the same time
always strictly respectful and well bred in his
conversation and in his manner. He treated the
milliner's assistant with as much courtesy as he
would bestow upon a duchess; and it was only in

his occasional colloquies with Madame Clarisse
that he permitted himself the use of phrases which
but few of his compatriots would have understood,
and which even in France would have been more
easily intelligible in the Rue de Bréda than in the
Faubourg St. Germain.

And what were Daisy's feelings towards Colonel
Orpington?   Did she really love or care for him?
Not one whit.

Had she forgotten Paul and all their long
walks and talks, all the devotion which he had
proffered her, all her acknowledgments of regard for him?   Had his image faded out of her
heart during his absence, and was it there re-
placed by another and less worthy one?   Not the
least in the world; only that the absence of her
lover had given the girl breathing space, as it
were, to look around her, and to estimate her
present position and her future chances at their
actual value.   And when thus seriously estimated,
she found that the devotion which Paul had proffered her was, to her thinking, not worth very
much; it was not sufficient to induce him to

pledge himself to marry her; it was not sufficient to induce him boldly to defy the opinion of the world, and break off those shackles of family and society by which he was bound hand and foot; it was only sufficient for him to give up a certain portion of his time to be passed in her company, which was after all a sufficiently selfish pleasure, as it pleased him as much as it did her. And then, after all, what was to be the result?

In the early days of their acquaintance, before he knew the character of the girl he had to deal with, Paul had given certain hints which Daisy had rigidly ignored, or when compelled to hear them, had forbidden to be repeated; but since then they had been going on in a vague purpose-less way; and though the boy-and-girl attachment, the stolen meetings, the letters, and the know-ledge that they loved each other, were in them-selves sufficient, and would last for ever, due con-sideration gave Daisy no clue to the probable result of that connection. And yet she loved Paul; had no idea how much she loved him until she was thinking over what her future, what a

portion of her future at least, might be if passed
with somebody else.

If passed with somebody else? There could
be no doubt about what was intended, though he
had never said a word, or given the slightest hint.
The conversation of her employer—who, as Daisy
was clear-headed and keen-witted enough to see,
was in the Colonel's confidence—was full of subtle
meaning. No need for the Frenchwoman to enlarge to Daisy on what she meant by the golden
opportunity; no need for her to dwell upon the
comforts and luxuries which were easily procur-
able by her—the dresses and equipages, the pomps
and vanities which so many wasted their lives in
endeavouring to obtain, and which might be hers
at once.

Hers; and with them what? A life of shame,
a career such as she had regarded always with
loathing and horror; such as she had told her
mother that, whatever temptation might assail her,
she had sufficient courage and strength of mind to
avoid. And such a life, not with a young lover,
the warmth of whose passion, whatever might be

its depth, it was impossible to deny, but with a man no longer young, who pretended to no sentiment for her beyond admiration, and who, polished, courteous, and gentlemanly as he was, would probably look upon her as any other appanage of his wealth and position, and care for her no more.

And yet, and yet were they to go on for ever—the long days of drudgery, the nights in the cheerless garret, the weary existence with the one ray of hope which illumined it, the love for Paul, soon necessary to be quenched for ever? She could not bear to think of that. Should she give it up, fling all to the winds, tell her lover on his return, which she was now daily expecting, that she could stand it no longer; bid him take her and do with her as he willed—marry her or not, as he chose, but let her feel that there was something worth living for, some bond of union which, legal or illegal, lessened the hard exigences of daily life, and took something of the grimness off the aspect of the world ?

She was mad! Was that to be the end of all her cultivated coldness and self-restraint? Had she

quietly, if not cheerfully, accepted the wretched
life which she had been leading so long, with the
one aim of establishing for herself a position, and
was she now going to undo all that she had so
patiently planned and so weariedly carried out in
one moment of headstrong passion ? Was the position which she hoped to acquire, for which she
had so earnestly striven, to prove to be that of
a poor man's mistress, where everything would
have been lost and nothing gained? Nothing
gained! Nothing? not Paul's love? No, she
had that now; and she was quite sufficient woman
of the world to know that in the chance of such a
contingency as she had contemplated, she might
not be long in losing it.

As the time for Paul Derinzy's return ap-
proached, Daisy became more and more unsettled.
It would seem as though Colonel Orpington had
been made aware of the speedily anticipated reappearance on the scene of one who might be
considered his rival; and, indeed, Miss Bella
Merton had been several times recently to Mr.
Wilson's chambers in the Temple, and held long

conversations with the occupant thereof. As he was more than usually assiduous in his attentions to Fanny, she, Madame Clarisse, had accompanied them once or twice to the theatre; and on one occasion, when the Frenchwoman had declared that Fanfan was dying for fresh air—it was one morning after the girl had passed a sleepless night in thinking over all the difficulties that beset her future, and she looked very pale and weary eyed—the Colonel had placed his brougham at the disposal of the ladies, and insisted on their driving down in it to Richmond, whither he proceeded on horseback, and had luncheon provided for them on their arrival at the hotel.

More assiduous, but not more particular beyond telling her laughingly one day that he should speedily ask her for an interview, at which he should ask her consent to a little project that he intended to carry out, the Colonel's conversation was of his usual ordinary light kind; but Madame Clarisse's hints were more subtle than ever, and Daisy could not fail to have some notion of what the project to be proposed at the suggested interview might be.

One Sunday morning—Paul was to come up from Devonshire that night, and had written her a wild letter full of rhapsodical delight at the idea of seeing her again the next day—Daisy was seated in her room.

Her little well-worn writing-desk was open, the paper was before her, the pen lay ready to her hand; but the girl was leaning back in her chair, and wondering how much or how little of the actual state of affairs she ought to describe in the letter to her mother which she was then about to write; for it had come to that, that there was concealment between them. Of her acquaintance with Colonel Orpington, Daisy had breathed never a word; while on her side Mrs. Stothard had carefully concealed the fact, that she was an inmate of the house which was the home of her daughter's lover, where at the time he was actually staying.

Daisy was roused from her deliberation by a rap at the door, and by the immediate entrance of

Mrs. Gillot her landlady, who told her that a gentleman wished to see her.

It was come at last then, this interview at which all was to be decided!

Daisy felt her face flush, and knew that Mrs. Gillot remarked it.

" A gentleman!" she repeated.

" Ay, a gentleman," said the worthy woman; " and one of the right sort too, or you may depend upon it I wouldn't have had him shown into my front parlour, where he now is. Not but what you can take care of yourself, Miss Fanny, and I trust you to give any jackanapes a regular good setting-down, with your quiet look, and your calm voice, and your none-of-your-impudence manner; but this is a gentleman, and when I showed him into the parlour, I told him I was sure you would see him."

" I will come directly, Mrs. Gillot."

She rose, took a hasty glance in the little scrap of looking-glass, and descended the stairs.

Her heart beat highly as she laid her hand upon the parlour-door. It resumed its normal rate of pulsation as the door opened beneath her touch, and she saw, standing before her on the hearth-rug, the unexpected figure of John Merton.

Something in her face when she first recognised him, something in the tone of her voice, some note of surprise and disappointment when she bade him good-morning, must have betrayed itself, for he said hurriedly :

"You did not expect to see me, Miss Stafford."

"I confess I did not ; but of course I am very glad. I—I hope Bella is quite well ?"

"Bella is very well, I believe."

"Have you brought me some message from her ?"

"No, indeed. She does not even know I was coming here."

There was a pause, then he said :

"I suppose you do not think I have taken a liberty in calling on you, Miss Stafford ?"

"O dear, no ! I have known you so long, and your sister is such an intimate acquaintance of mine, that it could not be anything of that sort. What makes you ask?"

"Well, you looked so—so surprised at seeing me."

"I was surprised at seeing any one. No one ever comes here after me."

"No?" said John Merton interrogatively, and his face seemed to brighten as he said it.

"No," said Daisy; "and my landlady must have been as much astonished as I am. You must have made a very favourable impression on her to obtain admittance."

"Mrs. Gillot is a very old friend of mine," said John Merton. "She has known me since I was a boy; but I should not have presumed upon that acquaintance to ask for you, nor indeed, Miss Stafford, should I have ventured to come here at all, if I had not something very particular to say to you."

"Very particular to say to me!"

"To say to you something so special and particular, that your answer to it may change the course of my whole life. I must ask you to listen to me, Miss Stafford. I won't keep you a minute longer than I can help."

Daisy bowed her head in acquiescence. She had taken a seat, but he remained standing before her, half leaning over towards her, with one hand on the table.

Poor John Merton! The girl's eyes rested on that hand, with its great thick red fingers and coarse knuckles and clumsy wrist; and then they travelled up the shiny sleeve of his black coat, and over his blue-silk gold-sprigged tie to his good-looking face shining with soap, and his jet-black hair glistening with grease. And then she dropped her eyes, and inwardly shuddered, comparing them with the hands and features of two other people of her acquaintance.

"You said just now," said John Merton, in rather a husky voice, "that you were not annoyed at my calling upon you, because you had known me so long, and because you were so intimate with my sister. I think I might allege those two reasons as the cause of my being here now. All the time I have known you I have had but one feeling towards you, and all that I have heard my sister say of you—and she seems never to be talking of anybody else—has deepened and concentrated that feeling. What that feeling is," continued John, "I don't think I need try to explain. I don't think I could if I tried, unless —unless I were to say that I would lay down my life to save you from an ache or a pain, that I worship the very ground you tread on, and that I look upon you like an angel from heaven!"

His voice shook as he said these words; but the fervour which possessed him lit-up his features; and as Daisy stole an upward glance at him, and saw his pleading eyes and working mouth, she forgot the homeliness of his appearance, and wondered how her most recent thoughts about him had ever found a place in her mind.

He caught something of her feeling, and said quickly, "You are not angry with me?"

She shook her head in dissent.

"You mustn't be that," he said, "whatever answer you may give me. I know how inferior I am to you in every possible way. I know, I can't help knowing, I couldn't help hearing even at that girl's the other evening, the last time we met, how you were noticed and admired by people in a very different position from mine : have known this and borne it all, and never spoken—shouldn't have spoken now, but that there is come a chance in my life which I must either accept or relinquish, and I want you to decide it for me."

" You want me to decide it !"

" You, and you alone can do it. This is how it comes about, Miss Stafford. You know I am what they call a ' counter-jumper,' " said he, with a little bitter laugh ; " but I know, that though it is a distinction without a difference, I suppose, to those who are not in the trade, I am one of the first hands with perhaps the largest silk-mercers in London, and I have been taken frequently abroad by one of the firm when he has gone to buy goods in a foreign market. I must have pleased them, I suppose, for now they are going to set-up an agency in Lyons ; and they have offered it to me, and I shall take it if you will come with me as my wife."

He paused, and Daisy was silent.

After a minute, he said hurriedly:

"You don't speak. It is not a bad thing pecuniarily. They would make it about three hundred a-year, I think, and I should get very good introductions, and it would be like beginning life again for both of us. I thought it would be a good chance of shaking-off any old associations; and as the position would be tolerable, it would be only me—myself, I mean—that you would have to put up with, and— You don't speak still! I haven't offended you?"

She looked up at him. Her face was very pale, and her hands fluttered nervously before her; but there was no break in her voice as she said:

"Offended me! You have done me the greatest honour in your power, and you talk about offence! You must not ask me for an answer now; I cannot give it; the whole thing has been so sudden. I will think it over, and write to you in a day or two at most. Meantime, I think it would be advisable for both our sakes that you should not speak of what has occurred, even to your sister."

" Of course not," he said; " anything you wish. And you tell me that I may hope ?"

" I did not quite say that," she said with a smile. " I told you you must wait for my reply. You shall have it very soon. Now, good-bye."

She held out her hand to him, and he took it in his own—which again looked horribly red and common, she thought—then he just touched it with his lips, and he was gone.

" Another element, a third element in the confusion," said Daisy to herself as she reascended the stairs to her room; " but one not so difficult to deal with as the others."

CHAPTER X.

IT was not likely that a man of George Wain-wright's intelligence and habits of observation could remain long domesticated in a household like that of the Derinzys', without speedily read-ing the characteristics of its various members.

In a very little time after his arrival, the young man—whose manners were so quiet and sedate as to lead Captain Derinzy to hint to his wife that he thought Wainwright rather a muff—had reckoned-up his host and knew exactly the amount of vanity, silliness, and ignorance which so largely swayed the estimable gentleman; had gauged Mrs. Derinzy's scheming worldliness, knew why it originated and at what it aimed; had thoroughly solved the problem, so difficult to all others, of Mrs. Stothard's position in the house; and knew exactly the character of the malady under which Annette was suffering.

He ought to have known more about Annette than about any body else, for nine-tenths of his time—all, indeed, that he could spare from the somewhat assiduous attentions of his host—were given to her. He walked with her, made long explorations of the neighbouring cliffs, long expeditions inland among the lovely Devonshire lanes, lovelier still with the fiery hue of autumn, and even induced her to join him and Paul in sundry boat-excursions, where, well wrapped up in rugs and tarpaulins, she lay on the flush-deck of the little fishing-smack, half frightened, half filled with child-like glee at her novel experience.

Paul had often laughed and said to their common associates, "When old George is caught, you may depend upon it, it will be a very desperate case."

And "old George" was caught now, Paul thought, and thought rightly: the delicacy, the good nature, the sweet womanly graces of the girl showing ever and anon between her sufferings—

for during George's stay at Beachborough, Annette had been free from any regular attack, yet from time to time there were threatenings of the coming storm which were perfectly perceptible to his experienced eye—nay, perhaps the very fact of the malady under which she laboured, and the position in which she was placed, had had strong influence over George Wainwright's honest heart. As for Paul, he was so thoroughly astonished at the change which had taken place in his cousin since George's arrival, and at the wonderful pains and trouble which George himself took to interest and amuse Annette, that this wonderment entirely filled so much of his time as was not devoted to thinking of Daisy. He wondered and pondered, and at last the conviction grew strong upon him, that George must be in love.

At first he laughed at the idea. The sober, steady, almost grave man, who had such large experience of life, and who yet had managed to steer clear, so far as Paul knew, of anything like a flirtation. Flirtation, indeed, would be the last thing to which his friend would stoop, " when

old George is caught." Something, perhaps, also—
" for pride attends us still"—was due to the fact
that Annette always showed the greatest desire
for his company, and undisguised delight at his
attention and admiration.   Never in the course of
her previous life had the girl met with any one
who seemed so completely to comprehend her,
whose talk she could so readily understand, whose
manner was so completely fascinating, and yet
somehow always commanded her respect.   She
despised her uncle, she disliked her aunt, and
hated Mrs. Stothard though she feared her ; but
in the slow and painful workings of that brain
she felt that if at those—those dreadful times when
semi-blankness fell upon her, and her perception
of all that was going on was dim, and obscure,
and confused,—if at such a time George Wainwright were to order her to do anything in oppo-
sition to the promptings of that devil, which on
those occasions possessed her, she felt she should
be powerless to disobey him.

    "I can't make it out, George; upon my soul,
I can't," said Paul, as they were walking along

the edge of the cliffs one morning, smoking their pipes after breakfast.

"What is it that puzzles your great brain, and that prompts to such strong utterances?" asked George, laughing.

"You know perfectly well what I mean. You needn't try to be deceitful in your old age," said Paul; "for deceit is a thing which I don't think you would easily learn, and at all events does not go well with hair which is turning white at the temples, and a beard which is beginning to grizzle, Mr. Wainwright. You know perfectly well that I am alluding to the attentions which you are paying to my cousin, Miss Derinzy. And I should be glad to know, sir," continued Paul, vainly endeavouring to suppress the broad grin which was spreading over his face,—"I should be glad to know, sir, how you reconcile your conduct with your notions of honour, knowing, as you perfectly well do, that that lady is my affianced bride."

"Don't be an ass, Paul," said George, smiling in his turn. "I dispute both your assertions, especially the last. The lady is nothing of the kind."

"No, poor dear child, that she certainly isn't. And I think on the whole that it is a very good thing that my affections are engaged in another quarter; for I am perfectly sure that, however much I might have wished it, Annette would never have had anything to say to me. I endeavoured to make my mother understand that, when she first talked to me on the subject when you first came down here; but she seemed to look upon Annette's wishes as having very little to do with the matter."

"Mrs. Derinzy's state of health possibly makes her take an exceptional view of affairs," said George, looking hard at his friend.

"Well, I declare I don't know about her state of health," said Paul. "I confess that, beyond a little peevishness, which is partly constitutional, I suppose, and partly brought on by having lived so many years with the governor,—good old fellow the governor, but an awful nuisance to have to be with constantly,—I don't see that there is

much the matter with my mother. Have you
ever heard your father say anything about her
illness, George?"

"My father is remarkably reticent in professional matters," said George. "I have never heard him speak about any illness in this
house."

"O, of course, it was only about my mother
that he could say anything," said Paul; "for the
governor never has anything the matter with him,
except a touch of sciatica now and then in his
game leg; and Annette's seems to be—you know
—one of those chronic cases which never come to
much, and which no doctor can ever do any good
to."

"I suppose you won't be sorry to get back to
town, Master Paul?"

"I suppose you will be sorry to leave here,
Master George? No; indeed, I am rather glad
the end of my leave is coming on; no intended
bad compliment to you, old fellow; your stay here
has been the greatest delight to me; but the fact
is, I am getting rather anxious about that young

person in London, and shall be very glad to see
her again."

George looked up at him with a comical face.

"You don't mean to say that since Theseus's
departure, Ariadne has—"

"I mean to say nothing of the sort," said
Paul, turning very red. "Daisy is the best girl
in the world; but I don't know, somehow I don't
think her letters have been quite as jolly lately—
the last two, I mean; there is something in them
which I can't exactly make out, and there is not
something in them which I have generally found
there; so that after all, as I said before, I shall
be glad when I get back."

"Has Mrs. Derinzy said anything more to
you on the subject which you wrote to me about?"
asked George, with a very bad attempt at indif-
ference.

"No," said Paul; "she has begun it once or
twice, but something has always intervened."

"Have you any idea that she has given up
her intention of getting you to marry Miss Annette?"

"I fear not; I fear that her intention remains just the same, and that I shall have an immense deal of trouble in combating it. You see, events have changed since your arrival here, my dear George. But speaking dispassionately together, I don't see what line I can take with my mother in declining to propose for Annette, except the straightforward one that I won't do it. It seems highly ridiculous for a man in a government office, and with only the reversion of a sufficiently snug, but certainly not overwhelming, income in prospect, to refuse the chance of an enormous fortune, and the hand of a very pretty girl, who, as Mr. Swiveller says, has been expressly growing up for me."

"Yes," said George reflectively, "I quite see what you mean; it will be a difficult task. But you intend to carry it through?"

"Most decidedly. Nothing would induce me to break with—with that young person in London; and if she were to break with me, God knows it would half kill me. I don't think I could solace myself by taking a wife with a lot of money, even if I could be such a ruffian as to attempt it."

So from this and fifty other conversations of a similar nature—for the theme was one which always engrossed his mind, and was constantly rising to his tongue—George Wainwright knew that there would be no obstacle to his love for Annette so far as Paul Derinzy was concerned. That young man had no care for his cousin even without the knowledge of the dreadful secret, which must be known to him some day, and the revelation of which would inevitably settle his resolution to decline a compliance with his mother's prayer.

That dreadful secret, always up-rearing its ghastly form in the path which otherwise was so smooth and so straight for George Wainwright's happiness! All his cogitations came to one invariable result—there could be no other explanation of it all. The illness which she herself could not explain, which came upon her from time to time, and during which she sank away from ordinary into mere blank existence, emerging therefrom with no knowledge of what she had gone through; the mysterious woman, half nurse, half keeper, who watched so constantly and so grimly over her; the manner in which all questions touching upon the girl's illness were shirked by every member of the household; the delusion so assiduously kept up, under which Mrs. Derinzy and not her niece was made to appear as the sufferer; above all, the constant visits of his father,—all these proved to George that the disorder under which Annette Derinzy laboured was insanity and nothing else.

And the more he thought of it, the more terrified was he at the idea. Familiarity with mental disease, intercourse with those labouring under it, had by no means softened its terrors to George Wainwright. True, he had no physical fear in connection with the mere vulgar fright which is usually felt with "mad people." He had no experience of that; but he had seen so much of the gradual growth of the disorder; had so often marked the helpless hopeless state into which those suffering under it fell—silently indeed, but

surely—that he had come to regard it with greater
terror than the fiercest fever or the deadliest
plague.

And now, when for the first time in his life
he had fixed his affections on a girl who seemed
likely to return his passion, and who in every
other way was calculated to form the charm of
his home and the happiness of his fireside, he
had to acknowledge to himself that she was af-
flicted with this dreadful malady. It was impossible to palter with the question; he had tried to
do so a thousand times; but his strong common
sense would not be juggled with. And there the
dread fact remained—the girl he loved was frequently liable to attacks of insanity. He must
face that, look at it steadily, and see what could
be done. Could she be cured?

Ah! how well he knew the futility of such a
hope! How many instances had he seen in his
father's house of patients whose disease was not
of nearly such long standing as Annette's, had
indeed only just begun, and who were in a few
days, or weeks, or months at the farthest, to be

restored, with all their faculties calmed and renewed, to their anxious friends!—and how many
of them remained there now, or had been removed
to other asylums, in the hope that change might
effect that restoration which skill and science had
failed in bringing about!

The last day of their stay had arrived, and on
the morrow George was to accompany his friend
back to London. The Captain was out for his
usual ramble, Paul was closeted with his mother,
and George was sitting in the little room which,
owing to the few books possessed by the family
gathered together in it, was dignified by the name
of a " study," and which overlooked a splendid view
of the bay. He was standing at the window, gazing out over the broad expanse of water, thinking
how strangely the usually calm-flowing current of
his life had been vexed and ruffled since his arrival there, wondering what steps he could take
towards the solution of the difficulty under which
he laboured, and what would be the final end of
it all, when he heard a door close gently behind
him, and looking round, saw Annette by his side.

"I am so glad I've found you, Mr. George," she said, looking up at him frankly, and putting out her hand (she always called him 'Mr. George' now; she had told him she hated to use his surname, it reminded her of disagreeable things),—"I am so glad I've found you. Mrs. Stothard reminded me that it was your last day here, and said I ought to make the most of it."

"Mrs. Stothard said that?" asked George, with uplifted eyebrows; "I would sooner it had been your own idea, Miss Annette."

"The truth is, I think I am a little vexed at the notion of your going," said the girl.

"Come, that is much better," said George, with a smile.

"No, no, I mean what I say; I am very, very sorry that you are going away." As she said this, her voice, apparently involuntarily, dropped into a soft caressing tone, and her eyes were fixed on him with an earnest expression of regard.

"It is very pleasing to me to be able to know that my presence or absence causes you any emotion," said George.

"I have been so happy since you have been here," said the girl; "you are so different from anybody else I have ever met before. You seem to understand me so much better than any one else, to take so much more interest in me, and to be so much more intelligible yourself: your manner is different from that of other people; and there is something in the tone of your voice which I cannot explain, but which perfectly thrills me."

"I declare you will make me vain, Annette."

"That would be impossible; you could not be vain, Mr. George, you are far too sensible and good. It is singular to see how wonderfully well I have been since you have been here. On the morning after your arrival I felt as though I were going to have one of my wretched attacks, and Mrs. Stothard said it was because I had talked too much, and been too much excited the previous evening; but it passed off; and though I don't think I have ever talked so much to any one in my life before, and certainly was never so interested in any one's conversation, there has been no recurrence of it, and I have been perfectly well."

The bright look had passed away from George's face, and he was regarding her now with earnest eyes.

" If I thought that had actually been accomplished by my presence, I should be happy indeed; more happy in expectation of the future than in thinking over the past."

" In expectation of the future !" repeated the girl, pondering over the words. " O yes, surely; you are going away now, but you will come again to walk with me, and to talk with me : and you are only going away for a time. How strange I never thought of this before !"

As she said these words she crept closer to him; and he, bending down, took her small white hand between his, and looked into her face with a long gaze of deep compassion and great love.

" Yes, Annette," he said, " I will come again, and I. hope before very long. You must understand that this time, these past few weeks, have been quite as happy to me as you say they have

been to you; that if you have found me different
from any one you have ever known, I, in my turn,
have never seen any one like you—any one in
whom I could take such interest, for whom I
could do so much."

He raised her hand to his lips and kissed it
tenderly, and at that moment the door opened,
and Paul entered hurriedly. He gave a short
low whistle as he marked the group before him,
then advancing hurriedly, he said,

"George, it is all over, my boy; the storm we
have been expecting so long has burst at last.
My mother and I have just had a very bad quarter
of an hour together."

During the foregoing conversation Mrs. Stothard, sitting in her room, heard the sound of the
spring-bell which was suspended over her bed;
the handle of this bell was in Mrs. Derinzy's
apartments, and it was only used under exceptional circumstances, such as at times of Annette's
illness, or when Mrs. Derinzy required instant
communication with the nurse.

Mrs. Stothard heard the sound, but seemed in

no way greatly influenced thereby; she looked up very calmly, saying to herself, "I suppose some climax has arrived; the departure of this young man was sure to bring it about. She has been fidgety lately, I have noticed, at the constant attention Mr. Wainwright has paid to Annette, and at the evident delight with which the girl has received the attentions. That bids fair to go exactly as I could have wished it. But there is some hitch in the other arrangement, I fear, from the little I could overhear of what he said to his friend the other day about Fanny; it must have been about Fanny, although he called her by some other name which I couldn't catch. He seemed nervously anxious about her, and appears to think that his absence from town has weakened her affection for him. That ought not to be, and that is not at all like Fanny's tactics; though there is something wrong, I fear, for I have not heard from her for some time, and her last letter was scarcely satisfactory. Yes, yes," she added impatiently, as the bell sounded again, "I am coming. It seems impossible for you, Mrs. Derinzy, to bear the burden of your trouble alone, even for five minutes."

When she entered the room, she found Mrs. Derinzy lying on the sofa with her head buried in the pillow; she was moaning and sobbing hysterically, and rocking her body to and fro.

"Are you ill?" asked Mrs. Stothard calmly. as she took up her position at the end of the sofa, and surveyed her mistress without any apparent emotion.

"Yes, very ill, very ill indeed—half broken and crushed," cried Mrs. Derinzy. "It is too hard, Martha, it is too hard to have to go through what I have suffered, and to have all one's hopes blighted by the wilfulness of one for whom I have toiled and slaved so hard and so long."

"You mean Mr. Paul," said Mrs. Stothard. "I suppose that, notwithstanding my strong advice to the contrary, you have persisted in your determination, and asked him, before leaving to return to London, to give his answer about your project?"

"Yes," sobbed Mrs. Derinzy, "I have. I

had him in here just now, and I went over it all
again.   I told him how, when I first heard of that
ridiculous will which his uncle Paul had made, I
determined that the fortune which ought to have
been left to my boy, should become his somehow
or other; how I had decided upon the marriage
with Annette; how for all these years I had
worked to compass it and bring it about; and how,
now the time had arrived when the marriage ought
to take place—"

"You didn't tell him anything about Annette's
illness?" asked Mrs. Stothard, interrupting.

"Of course not, Martha," said Mrs. Derinzy,
raising her head and looking angrily at the nurse;
"how could you ask such a ridiculous question?"

"It is no matter, he will know it soon enough,"
said Mrs. Stothard quietly.   "Well, he refused?"

"He did," said Mrs. Derinzy, again bursting
into tears, "like a wicked and ungrateful boy as
he is; he refused decidedly."

"Did he give any reason?" asked Mrs. Stothard.

"He said that he had other views and intentions," said Mrs. Derinzy. "He talked in a grand theatrical kind of way about some passion that he had for somebody, and his heart, and a vast amount of nonsense of that kind."

"He is in love with somebody else, then?" asked Mrs. Stothard, looking hard at her mistress.

"So I gather from what he said; but I wouldn't listen to him for a moment on that subject. I told him I would get his father to speak to him, and that I myself would speak to his friend Mr. Wainwright, who appears to me never to leave Annette's side."

"So much the better for the chance of carrying out your wishes," said Mrs. Stothard grimly.

"That is to a certain extent my doing; I knew that Mr. Wainwright would be appealed to in this matter, and I thought it advisable that he should have just as much influence with Annette as he has with Paul; not that I think you can in the least rely upon his recommending his friend to fall in with your views."

"You don't think he will?"

"I don't indeed. Though he has given no

sign, I should be very much astonished if he don't completely master the mystery of the girl's illness ; and if so, it is not likely he would recommend this scheme to his friend without showing him exactly the details of the bargain proposed."

"Bargain, indeed, Martha!"

"It is a bargain and nothing else, as you know very well, and you and I may as well call things by their plain names. What do you propose to do now?"

"I told Paul I would give him a couple of months in which to think it over finally ; at the end of that time we shall go to town for a few weeks, for I really believe Captain Derinzy will go out of his mind if we have not some change, and there will be no danger now in taking Annette with us.   Then Paul will have had ample time to discuss it with Mr. Wainwright, and on his decision will of course depend how our future lives are to be passed."

"If Mr. Paul is still obstinate, you think there will be no farther occasion to keep Miss Annette in seclusion?" asked Mrs. Stothard.

"Miss Annette will be nothing to me, then," said Mrs. Derinzy, "except that if she marries any one else without Captain Derinzy's consent, she loses all her fortune; and I will take care that that consent is not very easily given."

"That is a new element in the affair," said Mrs. Stothard to herself, as she walked back to her room; "but not one which is likely to prove an impediment to my friend the philosopher here."

CHAPTER XI.

NOTWITHSTANDING there was a most excellent un-
derstanding between George Wainwright and his
father, and as much affection as usually subsists
between men similarly related, they saw very little
of each other, although inhabiting, as it were,
the same house. They had scarcely any tastes or
pursuits in common. When not engaged in actual
practice, in study, or communicating the result of
that study to the world, Dr. Wainwright liked to
enjoy his life, and did enjoy it in a perfectly re-
putable manner, but very thoroughly. He read
the last new novel, and went to the last new play
of which people in society were talking ; he dined
out with tolerable frequency ; and took care never
to miss putting in an appearance at certain *salons,*

where the announcement of his name was heard with satisfaction, and at which the announcement of his presence in the next morning's newspaper was calculated to do him service.

The Doctor had the highest respect and a very deep regard for his son, whose acquirements he did not undervalue, but with whose tastes he could not sympathise; so it was that they comparatively very seldom met; and though on the occasions of their meeting there was always great cordiality on both sides, the relations between them were more those of friends than of kinsmen, more especially such nearly allied kinsmen as parent and child.

On the second evening after his return from Beachborough, George Wainwright dined at his club, and instead of going home, as was almost his invariable custom, turned up St. James's-street, with the intention of proceeding to his father's rooms in the Albany.

It was a dull muggy November night, and George shuddered as he made his way through the streets and walked into the hospitable arcade,

at the door of which the gold-laced porter stood
in astonishment at the unfamiliar apparition of
Dr. Wainwright's son.

"The Doctor's in, and alone, sir, I think,"
said he, in reply to George's inquiry. "The
same rooms, however—3 in Z; he has not moved
since you were last here."

George nodded, and passed on. On his arrival
at his father's rooms, which were on the first-
floor, he found the oak sported; but he knew that
this really meant nothing, it being the Doctor's
habit to show "out," as it were, against any chance
callers; while, if he were within, the initiated
could always obtain admission by a peculiar
knock. This knock George gave at once, and
speedily heard the sound of some one moving
within. Presently the doors were opened, and
Dr. Wainwright appeared on the threshold; he
held a reading-lamp in his hand, which he raised
above his head as he peered into the face of his
visitor.

"George!" he cried, after an instant's scru-
tiny, "this is a surprise. Come in, my dear boy.

How damp you are, and what a wretched night! Come in, and make yourself comfortable."

"I am not disturbing you, father, I hope?" said George, as he followed the Doctor into the room. "As usual, you are in the thick of it, I see," he continued, while pointing to a pile of books, some open, some closed, with special passages marked in them by pieces of paper hanging out of the edges, and to a mass of manuscript on the Doctor's blotting-pad.

"Not a bit, my dear boy, not a bit," said the Doctor; "I was merely demolishing old Dilsworth's preposterous theories as regards puerperal insanity. By the way, you should look at his pamphlet, George; you know quite sufficient of the subject to comprehend in an instant what an idiot he makes of himself; indeed I should be quite glad to escape from his unsound premises and ridiculous conclusions into the region of common sense."

"You are looking very well," said George; "your hard work does not seem to do you any harm."

"No, indeed, my dear boy; the harder I work,
the better I feel, I think; but I take a little more
relaxation than I did, and I like to have things
comfortable about me."

The Doctor gave a careless glance round the
room as he spoke. He certainly had things comfortable there: the paper was a dark green; all
the furniture was in black oak—not Wardour-
street, nor manufactured in the desolate region of
the Curtain-road in Shoreditch, but real black
oak, the spoil of country mansions whose owners
had gone to grief, and labourers' cottages, the
tenants of which did not know the value of their
possession, and were not proof against the blandishments of the Hebrew emissary, who was so
flattering with his tongue and so ready with his
cash. On the walls hung a large painting of a
nude figure by Etty, supported on either side by
a glowing landscape by Turner and a breezy sea-
scape by Stansfield. A noble old book-case stood
in one corner of the room, filled with literature
of all kinds—for the Doctor was an omnivorous
reader, and could have passed an examination as

to the characters and qualities of the three leading serials of the day, as well as in the secular and professional volumes which filled his lower shelves; while at the other end of the room a huge sideboard was covered with glass, from heavy *moyen-âge* Bohemian to the thinnest and lightest productions of the modern blower's art.

"What will you take?" asked the Doctor. "Like myself, you are not much of a drinker, I know; but, like myself, you understand and appreciate a little of what is really excellent. Now, on that sideboard there are sherry, claret, and brandy, for all of which I can vouch. A little of the latter with some iced water?—the refrigerator is outside. Nothing? Ah, I forgot, you are dying for your smoke after dinner. Smoke away here, my boy; no one ever comes to these chambers who would be frightened at the anti-professional odour; and as for me, I rather like the smell of a pipe, and especially delight in seeing your enjoyment of it; so fire away."

George lit his pipe, and both the men pulled their easy-chairs in front of the fire. There was an undeniable likeness between them in feature as well as in figure, though the elder man was so much more *soigné*, so much better got-up, so much better preserved than the younger.

"I have been away for some time," said George, after a few puffs at his pipe; "as perhaps you know."

"O yes, I found it out very soon after your departure, from the desolation which seemed to have fallen upon the house down yonder. Nurses and patients joined in one chorus of regret; and as for poor old Madame Vaughan, she seemed actually to forget the loss of the child she has been bewailing for so many years in her intense sorrow at your departure."

"Poor dear *maman!*" said George, with a smile; "I feared she would miss me and my nightly visits very much. It's so long since I went away, that I imagine I was regarded as a permanent fixture in the establishment."

"I confess I looked upon you in that light very much myself, George," said the Doctor, "and after your departure felt what Mr. Browning calls the 'conscience prick and memory smart' at not having previously asked why and where you were going. It is rather late to pretend any interest now you have returned, but still I would ask where you have been and why you went."

"I have been staying with some people who are friends of yours down in the west."

"Down in the west you have been staying?" said the Doctor. "Whom do I know down in the west? Penruddock—Bulteel—Holdsworth?"

"Not so far west as where those people you have just named live," said George. "I have been staying with the Derinzys."

"The Derinzys!"

And the Doctor's eyebrows went up into his large forehead, and his usually calm face expressed intense astonishment.

After a few minutes' pause, he said:

"Ah, I forgot. Young Derinzy is a colleague of yours, and a chum, I think I have heard you say."

"Yes; it was on his invitation I went down

to stay with his people. He was there on leave himself at the time."

"Ah!" said the Doctor, who had recovered his equanimity. "And what did you think of his people, as you call them?"

"They were very pleasant, kind, and unaffected, and thoroughly hospitable," said George. "Mrs. Derinzy is said to be in bad health. I understand that you have been occasionally summoned down there on consultation, sir?"

He looked hard at his father; but the Doctor's face was unmoved.

"Yes," he said quietly, "I remember having been down there once or twice."

"To visit Mrs. Derinzy?"

"I was sent for to visit Mrs. Derinzy."

George paused for a moment, then he said:

"I saw a good deal of a young lady who seems to be domesticated there—a niece of the family, as I understand—Miss Annette."

"Ah, indeed! You saw a good deal of Miss Annette? And what did you think of her?"

"I thought her charming. You have seen her?"

"O, yes, I have seen her frequently."

"And what is your impression?"

"The same as yours; Miss Annette is very charming."

The two men formed a curious contrast. George had laid by his pipe and was leaning over an arm of his chair, looking eagerly and scrutinisingly in his father's face; the Doctor lay back at his length, his comfortable dressing-gown wrapped around him, his slippered feet on the fender, his eyes fixed on the fire, while he gently tapped the palm of one hand with an ivory paper-knife which he held in the other.

"Father," said George Wainwright, suddenly rising and standing on the rug before the fire, "I want to talk to you about Annette Derinzy."

"My dear George," said the Doctor, without changing his position, "I shall be very happy to talk to you about any inmate of that house; always respecting professional confidences recollect, George."

"You must hear me to the end first, sir, and then you will see what confidences you choose to

give to, and what to withhold from, me. Whatever may be your decision I shall, of course,
cheerfully abide by; but it is rather an important matter, as you will find before I have
finished, and I look to you for assistance and
advice in it."

There was such an earnestness in the tone in
which George spoke these last words, that the
Doctor raised himself from his lounging position
and regarded his son with astonishment.

"My dear boy," said he, putting out his hands
and grasping his son's warmly, "you may depend
on having both to the utmost extent of my power.
We don't see much of each other, and we don't
make much parade of parental and filial affection;
but I don't think we like each other the less for
that; and I know that I am very proud of you,
and only too delighted to have any opportunity—
you give me very few—of being of service to you.
Now speak."

"You never told me you knew the Derinzys,
father."

"My dear boy, I don't suppose I have ever

mentioned the names of one third of the persons whom I know professionally in your hearing."

" But you knew Paul was my friend."

" Exactly," said the Doctor, with a smile, "and in my knowledge of that fact you might perhaps find the reason of my silence."

" Ah !" said George, " of course I see now; it is no use beating about the bush any longer; I must come to it at last, and may as well do so at once. You will tell me, won't you? Is Annette Derinzy mad ?"

The Doctor was not the least disturbed by the question, nor by the excited manner—so different from George's usual calm—in which it was put. He looked up steadily as he replied,

" Yes ; I should say decidedly yes, in the broad and general acceptation of the word ; for people are called mad who are occasionally subjects of mental hallucination, and at other times are remarkably clear - sighted and keen - witted. Miss Derinzy is one of these."

" Have you attended her ?"

" For some years."

" And she has always been subject to these attacks ? "

" Ever since I knew her. I was, of course, at first called in to her on account of them."

" Your attendance on Mrs. Derinzy has been merely a pretext ? "

" Exactly ; a pretext invented by the family, and not by me."

" Have you any reason for imagining why this pretext was made ? "

" They wished to keep every one in ignorance of Miss Derinzy's state, and asked me to procure a trustworthy person whom I could recommend as her nurse—"

" Ah, Mrs. Stothard ? "

" Exactly ; Mrs. Stothard—you have made her acquaintance too ?—and to visit the young lady from time to time."

" And you were asked to keep the fact of your visits from me ? "

" Certainly. The Derinzys were aware that you were in the same office with their son, and were most desirous that his cousin's state should be concealed from him, above all others. Why, I never thought proper to inquire."

"I know the reason," said George with half a sigh. "Do you think that this dreadful disease under which Miss Derinzy suffers is progressing or decreasing?"

"I am scarcely in a position to say," said the Doctor. "Were she in London, or in any place easy of access, I should be better able to judge; but now I only visit her periodically, and even that by no means regularly, merely when I have a day or two which I can steal, so that I cannot judge of the increase or decrease, or of the extent of delirium. However, the last time I was there— yes, the last time—I happened to be present when one of the attacks supervened, and it was very strong, very strong indeed."

There was another pause, and then the Doctor said lightly,

"I think I may put you into the 'box' now, George, and ask you a few questions. You saw a great deal of Miss Derinzy, you say?"

"Yes, we were together every day."

"And you deduced your opinion of her mental state from your observation of her?"

"Not entirely."

"Of course you got no hint from any of the family, not even from Captain Derinzy himself, who is sufficiently stupid and garrulous?" said the Doctor, with a recollection of his last visit to Beachborough, and the familiarity under which he had writhed.

"No, from none of them; and certainly not from Miss Derinzy's manner, which, though unusually artless and child-like, decidedly bore no trace of insanity."

"But, my dear boy, you must have had your suspicions, or you would not have asked me the questions so plainly. How did these suspicions arise?"

"From Annette's description of her illness— of her symptoms at the time of attack, the blank which fell upon her, and her sensations on her recovery; from the mere fact of Mrs. Stothard's presence there—itself sufficient evidence to any one accustomed to persons of Mrs. Stothard's

class—and from words and hints which Mrs. Stothard—whether with or without intention, I have
never yet been able to determine—occasionally let
drop; from other facts which accidentally came to
my knowledge, but of which I think you are ig-
norant, and which I think it is not important
that you should know."

"For a superficial observer you have made a
remarkable diagnosis of the case, George," said
the Doctor, regarding his son with calm appreciation; "it is a thousand pities you did not take to
the profession."

"Thank God, I didn't," said the son; "even
as it is I have seen enough of it—or, at least, I
should have said 'Thank God' two months ago:
now, I almost wish I had."

"You would like to have taken up this case?"

"I should."

"You would like to have cured your friend's
cousin?"

"I should indeed!"

"My dear George," said the Doctor with a
smile, "I think, as I just said, it is a great

pity that you did not take up the profession. You have a certain talent, and great powers of reading the human mind, but you are given to desultory studies and pursuits; and your picture-painting, piano-playing, and German philosophy, all charming as they are, would have led you away from the one study on which a man in our profession must concentrate his every thought. I don't think, my dear George, that you would have been a better —well, what common people call a better 'mad doctor' than your father; I don't think the 'old man' would have been beaten by the 'boy' in this instance."

"I am sure not, sir; I never thought that for an instant: it was not that which prompted me to say what I did. Do I understand from your last remark that Miss Derinzy's disease is beyond your cure?"

"In my opinion, beyond any one's cure, my dear George."

"God help me!" And George groaned and covered his face with his hands.

The Doctor sprang to his feet, and stepping

across to where George sat, laid his hand tenderly on his head.

"My dear boy," said he, " my dear George, what does all this mean ?"

" Nothing, father," said George, raising his head and shaking himself together as it were. " Nothing, father—nothing, at least, which should lead a man to make a fool of himself; but your last words were rather a shock to me, for I love Annette Derinzy, and I had hoped—"

" You love Annette Derinzy ! You, whom we have all laughed at so long for your celibate notions, to have fallen in love now, and with Annette Derinzy ! My poor boy, this is a bad business—a very bad business indeed. I don't see what is to be done to comfort you."

" Nor I, father, nor I. You distinctly say there is no hope of her cure ?"

" Speaking so far as I can judge, there is none. If she were under my special care for a certain number of weeks, so that I saw her daily —Bah ! I am talking as I might do to the friends of a patient. To you, my dear George, I say it would be of no use. It is a horrible verdict, but a true one—she can never be cured."

George was silent for a minute, then he said:

"Would there be any use in having a consultation?"

"My dear boy, not the slightest in the world. I will meet any one that could be named. If this were a professional case, I should insist on a consultation, and the family apothecary would probably call in this old fool whose pamphlet I am just reviewing—Dilsworth, I mean, or Tokeley, or Whittaker, or one of them; but I don't mind saying to my own son, that I am perfectly certain I know more than any of these men of my peculiar subject, and that, except for the mere sake of differing, they always in such consultations take their cue from me."

Another pause; then George said, his face suddenly lighting up:

"One moment, sir. I have some sort of recollection, when I was a student at Bonn, hearing of some German doctor who had achieved a marvellous reputation for having effected certain cures in insane cases which had been given up by every one else."

"You mean old Hildebrand of Derrendorf," said the Doctor. "Yes, he was really a wonderful man, and did some extraordinary things. I never met him; but his cases were reported in the medical journals here, and made a great sensation at the time; but that is ten or twelve years ago, and I recollect hearing since that he had retired from practice. I should think by this time he must be dead."

"Then there is no hope," said George sadly.

"I fear none," said his father. "If Hildebrand were alive, there would be no chance of his undertaking the case; for if I recollect rightly, he had always determined on retiring from the profession as soon as he had amassed a certain amount of money, which would enable him to pursue his studies in quiet. He was an eccentric genius too, —one of the rough-and-ready school, they said, and particularly harsh and unpleasant in his manners. I recollect there was a joke that he frightened people into their wits, as other patients were

frightened out of theirs by their doctors ; so that
he would scarcely do for Miss Annette, even if
we could command his services. By the way, of
course there was no seizure while you were in the
house ?"

"Nothing of the kind. She was, as I said,
perfectly calm and tranquil, and wonderfully
artless and childlike."

"Yes ; she remains the ruin of what would
have been a most charming creature. That 'little
rift within the lute,' as Tennyson has it, has
marred all the melody. By the way, you said you
knew the reason of Mrs. Derinzy's having impressed upon me the necessity of silence in regard
to my visits there. What was it ?"

"There is no secret in it now. Mrs. Derinzy
always intended that her son Paul should marry
his cousin."

"I see it all! An heiress, is she not, to an
enormous property ? A very good thing for her
son."

"Ah! that was why, ever since symptoms of
the girl's mental malady first began to develop

themselves, the boy was kept away at school, even during the holidays, on some pretence or another; and why, since he has been at the Stannaries Office, he has, up to this time, always gone abroad or to stay with some friends on his leave of absence."

"Exactly. The secret has been well kept from him. And do you mean to say he does not know it now?"

"At this moment he hasn't the least idea of it."

"Then your friend is also your rival, my poor George?"

"No, indeed. Paul does not care in the least for Annette, and he is deeply pledged in another quarter. It was with a view of aiding him in extricating himself from the engagement which his mother was pressing upon him that he asked me down to the Tower."

"As neat a complication as could possibly be," said the Doctor.

"There is only one person whose way out seems to me tolerably clear," said George, "and

that is Paul. See here, father; I am neither of
an age nor of a temperament to rave about my
love, or to make much purple demonstration about
anything. I shall not yet give up the idea that
Annette Derinzy can be cured of the mental
disease under which she suffers; and in saying
this, I do not doubt your talent nor the truth of
what you have said to me; but I have a kind of
inward feeling that something will eventually be
done to bring her right, and that I shall be the
means of its accomplishment. I would not take
this upon myself unless my position were duly
authorised. I need not tell you—I am your son
—that nothing would induce me to move in the
matter, if my doing so involved the least breach
of loyalty to Paul, the least breach of faith to his
father or mother; but before I take a single step,
I shall get from him a repetition of his decision,
already twice or thrice given, in declining to become a suitor for Annette's hand; and armed
with this, I shall seek an interview with his
father and mother, and explain his position and
my own."

"And then ?" said the Doctor, with a grave face.

"And then, *qui vivra verra*."

"Well, George," said his father, laying his hand affectionately again on his son's head, "you know I wish you God speed. You have plenty of talent and endurance and pluck; and Heaven knows, you will have need of them all."

CHAPTER XII.

L'HOMME PROPOSE.

ONE morning in the early winter, Colonel Orpington walked into the Beaufort Club, and taking
his letters from the hall-porter as he passed, entered the coffee-room, and took possession of the
table which for many years he had been accustomed to regard as almost his own.

There was no occasion for him to order any
breakfast, so well were his ways known in that
establishment, of which he was not merely one
of the oldest, but one of the most conspicuous of
the members. The officers of the household, from
Riboulet the *chef* and Woodman the house-
steward down to the smallest page-boys, all held
the Colonel in very wholesome reverence; and
amongst the twelve hundred members on the

books, the behests of none were more speedily obeyed than his.

While the repast was preparing, Colonel Orpington glanced over the envelopes of the letters which he had taken from the porter and laid on the table in military order before him. They are many and various: heavy official-looking letters, thin-papered missives from the Continent, and two or three delicate little notes. The Colonel selects one of these last, which is addressed in an obviously foreign hand, though bearing a London post-mark; the others are put aside; the dainty double-eyeglasses are brought from their hiding-place inside his waistcoat and adjusted across his nose, and he falls to the perusal of the little note. A difficult hand to read apparently, for the Colonel, though somewhat careful of showing any symptoms of loss of sight to the more youthful members of the club then present, by whom he has a certain suspicion he is looked upon as a fogey, has to hold it in various lights and twist it up and down before he can master its contents. When he has mastered them they do not appear to be of a particularly reassuring character; for the Colonel shakes his head, utters a short low whistle, and is stroking his chin with his hand, as though deep in thought, when the advanced guard of his breakfast makes its appearance.

" ' Coming back at once,' " says the Colonel to himself; "at least, so far as I can make out Clarisse's confoundedly cramped handwriting. ' Coming back at once,' and from what she can make out from Fanny's talk, not in the best of tempers either, and likely to bring matters to an end; and Clarisse thinks I must declare myself at once. Well, I don't see why not.

" 'Gad, it seems to me an extraordinary thing that I, who have been under fire so many times in these kind of affairs, should have been hesitating and hanging back and beating about the bush for so long with this girl! To be sure, she is quite unlike many of the others; more like a person in society, or rather, like what used to be society in my time: what goes by that name now is a very

different thing. There's a sort of air of breeding about her, and a kind of *noli me tangere* sort
of thing mixed up with all her attractiveness, that
makes the whole business a very different thing
from the ordinary throwing the handkerchief and
being happy ever after.

"Coming back, eh! My young friend Derinzy — member here, by the way; letters had
better go to one of the other clubs in future; it
is best to be on the safe side. Coming back,
eh! And now what are — what parents call —
his 'intentions,' I wonder. Scarcely so 'strictly
honourable' as the middle-class father longs to
hear professed by enamoured aristocrats. If he
meant marriage, he would certainly have proposed
before he left town, when, if all I learn is true,
he was so wildly mad about the girl, he would
not have left her to— And yet, perhaps, that is
the very reason, though she said nothing, she
has evidently been pleased by the attentions which
I have shown her; and this perhaps has caused
her to slack off in her correspondence with this
young fellow, or to influence its warmth, or some-

thing of that kind, and this may have had the effect of bringing him to book.

"If he were to declare off, how would that suit me? Impossible to say. In the fit of rage and disgust with him, she might say yes to anything I asked her; on the other hand, she might have a fit of remorse, and think that it was all from having listened to the blandishments of this serpent she lost a chance of enjoying a perpetual paradise with that bureaucratic young Adam.

"There is the other fellow, too—the young man 'in her own station of life' — shopkeeper, mechanic, whatever he is. Clarisse seems to have some notion that he is coming to the fore, though I don't think there is any chance for him. The girl's tastes lie obviously in quite a different line, and I am by no means certain that his being in the race is a bad thing for me. However, it's plainly time that something must be done; and now, how to do it?"

He threw down his napkin before him as he spoke and rose from the table. The young men who had been breakfasting near him, though perhaps they might have thought him a fogey, yet envied the undeniable position he held in society; envied him, above all, the perfect freshness and good health and the evident appetite with which he had just consumed his meal, while they were listlessly playing with highly-spiced condiments, or endeavouring to quench the flame excited by the previous night's dissipation with effervescing drinks. Sir Coke Only, the great railway contractor and millionaire, whose neighbouring table was covered with prospectuses and letters on blue paper, propounding schemes in which thousands were involved, envied the Colonel that consummate air of good-breeding which he, the millionaire, knew he could never acquire, and that happy idleness which never seemed in store for him. The perfectly-appointed brougham, with its bit-champing, foam-tossing gray horse, stood at the club-door, waiting to whirl the man of business into the City, where he would be unceasingly occupied till dusk; "while that feller," as Sir Coke remarked to himself, "will be lunching with marchionesses and dropping into the five-o'clock tea with duchesses, and taking it as easy as though he were as rich as Rothschild."

Perhaps the Colonel knew of the envy which he excited; he was certainly not disturbed, and perhaps even pleased, by it. He sauntered quietly into the waiting-room, walked to the window, and stood gazing unconsciously at the black little London sparrows hopping about in the black little bit of ground which was metropolitan for a garden, and lay between the club and Carlton-house-terrace, while he collected his thoughts. Then he sat down at a table and wrote as follows:

" *Beaufort Club, Tuesday.*

"DEAR MISS STAFFORD, — The opportunity which I have been so long waiting for has at length arrived, and I think I see my way to the fulfilment of the promise made to you in the beginning of our acquaintance.

"If you will be at my lawyer's chambers, No. 5 Seldon-buildings, Temple, at two o'clock this afternoon, he—Mr. John Wilson is his name—will enter into farther particulars with you. I shall hear from him how he has progressed, and you will see me very shortly.—Very sincerely yours, JOHN ORPINGTON.

"P.S.—I have no doubt that Madame Clarisse will be able to spare you on your mentioning that you have business. You need not particularise its nature."

Then he wrote another letter consisting of one line :

"All right ; let her go.—J. O."

He addressed these respectively to Miss Fanny Stafford and Madame Clarisse, and despatched them to their destination.

It was with no particular excess of pleasure that Daisy received and perused the first-written of these epistles. To be sure, at the first glance over the words her face flushed and her eyes brightened ; but the next few minutes her heart sank within her with that undefined sense of impending evil of which we are all of us so frequently conscious. The thought of Paul's im-

mediate return had been weighing upon her for
some days; she had been uncertain how to treat
him.   She could not help acknowledging to herself that her feelings towards him had undergone
a certain amount of alteration during his absence.
She was unwilling that that alteration should be
noticed by him, and yet could not avoid a lurking suspicion that she must have betrayed it in
her letters.   She gathered this from the tone of
his replies, more especially from his last communication, in which he announced his speedy
arrival in town.   Of course she had not breathed
to him   one   word   of her   acquaintance   with
Colonel Orpington; there was   no occasion why
she should have done so, she argued to herself;
the two men would never be brought in contact.
And yet it would be impossible for her to renew
the intimacy which had previously existed with
Paul, without his becoming aware that she had
other calls upon her time, and insisting upon
being made acquainted with their nature; and
then, when he found it out, the fact of her having
concealed this newly-formed friendship from him

would tell very badly against her. It would have
been very much better that she should have mentioned it, giving some sufficiently satisfactory
account of its origin, and passing over it lightly
as though it were of no moment. She could have
done this in regard to the meeting with John
Merton and its subsequent results—not that she
had ever said anything of that to her lover, by
the way—without, she was sure, exciting Paul's
suspicion; but this was a different matter. In
his last letter Paul had proposed to meet her on
what would now be the next afternoon, and by
that time she must have made up her mind fully
as to the course she intended to pursue. The
interview to which she was then proceeding might
perhaps have an important effect upon her resolution. And as she thought of that interview
her heart sank again, and her face became very
grave and thoughtful; so grave and thoughtful
did she look as she hurried along one of the dull
streets in the neighbourhood of Russell-square,
that a man to whom she was well known, and
by whom every expression of her face was trea-

sured, scarcely knew her, as, coming in the opposite direction, he encountered and passed by
her. She did not notice him; but he turned,
and in the next instant was by her side. She
looked up; it was John Merton.

"You were walking at such a pace and looking so earnest, Miss Stafford," said he, after the
first ordinary salutations, "that I scarcely recognised you. You are going into the City. May
I walk part of the way with you? I am so glad
to see you; I have been longing so anxiously to
hear from you."

This was an awkward *rencontre*. Daisy had
quite sufficient mental excitement with the interview to which she was proceeding. She had
not calculated upon this addition to it, and ans-
wered him vaguely and unsatisfactorily.

"I have been very much occupied of late,"
said she. "The winter season is now coming
upon us, you see, and I have scarcely any time
to myself."

"It would have taken very little time to write
yes or no," said poor John; "and if you knew

the importance I attach to the receipt of one of those two words from you, I think you would have endeavoured to let me know my fate. Will you let me offer you my arm?"

"No—no, thanks," said Daisy, drawing back.

"You—you don't like to be seen with me, perhaps, in the street?" asked John, with a bitter tone in his voice.

"No, not that at all; only people don't take arms nowadays, don't you know?"

"Don't they?" said John, still bitterly. "I beg your pardon; you must excuse my want of breeding. I don't mix except among people in my own station. I — I didn't mean that," he added hurriedly, as he saw her face flush; "I didn't mean anything to offend you; but I have scarcely been myself, I think, for the last few days."

"You have done no harm," said Daisy gently, pitying the look of misery on his face.

"Have I done any good?" he asked; "you cannot fail to understand me. If you knew how I suffer, you would keep me no longer in suspense."

"I did not pretend to misunderstand you,"

said the girl. "You are waiting for my answer to the proposition you made to me when you called at my lodgings the other day."

"I am."

"You have placed me—unwillingly, I know—in a very painful position," said Daisy; "for it is really painful to me to have to say or do anything which I feel would give you pain."

"Don't say any more," he said in a hoarse voice; "I can guess your meaning perfectly. Don't say any more."

"But, Mr. Merton, you must hear me—you must understand—"

"I do understand that you say 'no' to what I asked you; that you reject my suit—I believe that is the proper society phrase! I don't want to know," continued he, with a sudden outburst of passion, "of the esteem in which you hold me, and the recollection which you will always have of the delicacy of my behaviour towards you. I know the rubbish with which it is always thought necessary to gild the pill in similar cases; but I'd rather be without it."

"You are becoming incoherent, and I can scarcely follow you," said Daisy, setting her lips, and looking very stony. "I don't think I was going to say anything of the kind that you seem to have anticipated. I don't see that I have laid myself open to rudeness because I have been compelled to tell you it didn't suit me to marry you; and as to our being friends hereafter, I really don't think that there is the remotest chance of such a thing."

"I must again beg your pardon, Miss Stafford," said John, taking off his hat—he was quite calm now—"and I will take care that I don't commit myself in any similar ridiculous manner. I am perfectly aware that our lines in life lie very wide apart, and after the decision which you have arrived at and just communicated to me, I can only be glad that it is so; and though we are not to be friends, you say, I shall always have the deepest regard for you. You cannot prevent that, even if you would; and I only trust that some day I may have the chance of proving the continuance of that regard by being able to serve you."

He stopped, bowed, and was striding rapidly back on the way they had traversed, before Daisy could speak to him.

"More quickly over than I had anticipated," she thought to herself, "and less painful, too. I expected at one time there would have been a scene. His face lights up wonderfully when he is in earnest, and if his figure and manner were only as good, he might do. I wonder whether I could put up with him if neither of those two other men had been upon the cards; perhaps so, in a foreign place, such as he talked of going to, where one could have made one's own world and one's own society, and broken with all the old associations. How dreadful his boots were, by the way! I don't think it would have been possible to have passed one's life recognised as belonging to such feet and boots."

By this time she had reached Middle Temple-lane, down which she was proceeding, to the great admiration of the barristers' and attorneys' clerks who were flitting about that sombre neighbourhood. After a little difficulty and a great deal of inquiry she found the Seldon-buildings ; and arriving at the second floor, and knocking at the portal inscribed with the name of Mr. John Wilson, she rather started when the door was opened to her by Colonel Orpington.

" Pray step in, my dear Miss Stafford," said the Colonel. "You are surprised, I see, to see me here instead of my legal adviser; but the fact is, that gentleman has been called out of town, and as I find he is not likely to return, I thought it best to take his place and make the proposition in my own person."

Daisy was not, nor did she feign to be, astonished. She entered the room and seated herself in an arm-chair, towards which the Colonel motioned her. He sat down opposite to her, and without any preliminary observations, at once dashed into his subject.

"I don't think there is any occasion for me to inform you, my dear Miss Stafford," he commenced, " that I have the very greatest admiration for you. All women know intuitively when they are admired without having the sentiment duly expressed to them in set phrases; and though I have carefully avoided saying or doing any of those ridiculous things which are said and done in novels and plays, but never in real life, except by people who bring actions of breach of promise against each other, you can have had very little doubt of the high appreciation of you which I entertain."

Daisy bowed. The trembling of her lip showed that she was a little nervous—no other sign.

" Well," continued the Colonel, " this admiration and appreciation naturally induced me to think what I could do to better your position, and at the same time to see more of you myself. Your life is not a particularly lively one—in fact, there is no doubt it is deuced hard work, and very little relaxation. You are not meant for this kind of thing. You like books, and flowers, and birds, and all sorts of elegant surroundings. You are so handsome—pardon the reference, but I am talking in a most perfectly business manner—that it is a thorough shame to see you lacking all those et ceteras which are such a help and set-off to

beauty; and you are wearing away the very flower
of your youth in what is nothing more nor less
than sordid drudgery. At one time I thought—
as I believe I mentioned to you—of purchasing
some business, such as that in which you are now
engaged, and putting you at the head—making
yourself, in point of fact, and placing you in the
position occupied by Madame Clarisse. But after
a good deal of reflection, I have come to the conclusion, and I think you will agree, that there
would not be much good in such a project. You
see, though you would be your own mistress, and
would not be obliged to get up so early or to work
so late, you would still be engaged in exactly the
same kind of employment; you would be at the
mercy of the caprices of horrible old women and
insolent young girls, and would have to fetch and
carry, and bow to, and eat humble-pie, and all
the rest of it, very much as you do at present.
And I am perfectly certain, my dear Fanny,"—
she gave a little start, which had not passed un-
noticed; it was the first time he had called her
so,—"I am perfectly certain that this is not your

métier. You are a lady in looks — there is no higher-bred-looking woman goes to Court, by Jove! — in education, in manner, and in taste ; you are not meant for contact with the shopocracy, and it wouldn't suit you ; and to tell you the truth, I am sufficiently selfish to have thought how it would suit me, and I confess I don't see it at all."

He looked hard at her as he said this, and she returned his glance. Her colour rose, and her lips trembled visibly.

"I am perfectly candid with you, my dear child," said the Colonel, drawing his chair a little closer to her, and leaning with his elbow on the table so as to bring his face nearer to her—"I am perfectly candid in avowing a certain amount of selfishness in this matter. I admire you very much indeed, and the natural result is, a desire to see as much of you as is consistent with my duties to society ; and this shopkeeping project wouldn't help me at all. I want you to have all your time to yourself—a perpetual leisure, to be employed according to your own devices. I wish you to have the prettiest home that can be found, with pictures, and books, and flowers, and such-like. I wish you to have your carriage, and a riding-horse, if you would like one, and a maid to attend to you, and a proper allowance for dress and all that kind of thing. You look incredulous, Fanny, and as though I were inventing a romance. It is perfectly practicable and possible, my dear child, and it shall all be done for you if you will only like me just a little."

He bent forward and took her hand, and looked up eagerly into her face.

She suffered her hand to remain in his grasp, and gazed at him quite steadily as she said in hard tones :

"It sounds like a fairy-tale ; but it is in fact a mere business-like proposition skilfully veiled. You wish me to be your mistress."

Colonel Orpington was not staggered either by the tone or the words, but smiled quietly, still holding her hand as he said :

"I told you I admired your appreciation and quickness, though I wish to Heaven you had not used that horrible word. I never had a mistress in my life. I always associate the term with a dreadful person with painted cheeks and blackened eyelids, and a very low-necked dress. I can't conceive any object more utterly revolting."

"I am sorry you dislike the term," said Daisy, "but I conclude I expressed your meaning."

"It would be better put thus," said the Colonel : "I wish you to let me be your lover, and show my regard by attending to your comfort and happiness. That seems to me rather neatly put."

Daisy could not help smiling as she said :

"It is certainly less startling in that shape."

"My dear child," said the Colonel, releasing her hand, and standing upright on the hearth-rug before her, "it conveys exactly what I meant to say. A young man would rave and romp, and swear he had never loved any one before, and would never love any one again. I can't say the first, by Jove!" said the Colonel, with a grin ; "and I could not take upon myself to swear to the last, we are such creatures of chance and circumstances. But it wouldn't matter to you, for by that time you would probably be tired of me, and I should take care to have secured your independence; but at all events I should be very kind to you, and you would have pretty well your own way."

There was a pause, after which the Colonel said:

"You are silent, Fanny; what do you say?"

"You cannot expect me," said Fanny, rising from her chair, "to give a decided 'Yes' or 'No' to this proposition of yours, however delicately you may have veiled it. You see I am as candid with you as you were with me. You have had no shrieks of horror, no exclamations of startled propriety, and I conclude you did not expect them; but it is a matter which I must think over, and let you know the result."

"Exactly what I expected from your common sense, my dear child. My appreciation of you is higher than ever. When shall I hear?"

"If I don't write to you before, I will be here this day-week at this time."

"So be it," said the Colonel, and he led her

to the door.   As she passed, he touched her fore-head with his lips, and so they parted.

"I suppose I ought to be in a whirl of terror, fright, and shame," said Daisy to herself, as she walked towards the West; "but I feel none of these sensations.   It is a matter which will require a great deal of thinking about, and must have very careful attention."

END OF VOL. II.

LONDON:
ROBSON AND SONS, PRINTERS, PANCRAS ROAD, N.W

www.ingramcontent.com/pod-product-compliance
Lightning Source LLC
Chambersburg PA
CBHW030811020726
47499CB00006B/1863

* 9 7 8 3 3 3 7 2 1 3 6 0 2 *